Living Past the Memories

Published by Hannah Sellars
Publishing partner: Paragon Publishing, Rothersthorpe
First published 2010
© Hannah Sellars 2010

ISBN 978-1-899820-94-8

Book design, layout and production management by Into Print
www.intoprint.net

Printed and bound in UK and USA by Lightning Source

Prologue

Chelsey was sitting at the dining room table reading a short letter she had just received in the post. She didn't quite know whether to believe what she was reading. It was signed 'Jackie Ryan', the name of her birth mother. Chelsey was under the impression that her real mum was dead, hence the reason why she had been shipped from orphanage to foster care and back again for the last 17 years. The letter had given her quite a shock.

"Chelsey, you've gone very pale, is it bad news?" Annie asked, as she sewed sequins onto the latest wedding dress she was making.

"It's from my mother, she wants to meet me."

Annie put down the dress and reached for the letter Chelsey was handing her. Quickly reading it she handed it back and after a moment she said, "Well this is a pleasant surprise. You don't look so sure about it?"

Chelsey didn't say anything for a while. She re-read the letter again and again trying to make some kind of sense of it. She had been an orphan all her life, grew up in an orphanage in Liverpool, shipped to different foster homes until one day she couldn't take it any longer and she ran away. She had met up with Jason who was also an orphan and they had decided to run away to London and make their fortunes. While Jason was caught trying to get a free train ride she had managed to hide in the toilet and ended up living on the streets of London for the next three years. By the time she made her way back to Liverpool Jason had been adopted. Eventually Jason's adoptive parents, Phil and Annie, became her foster parents. She had felt like she was part of a family now.

"I don't know what to think. Why didn't she turn up ten years ago when I wanted a mother? Why now? Just when I'm sort of getting my head sorted, she has to turn up and mess everything up."

"But honey she only wants to meet you. She isn't asking you to go and live with her. Maybe what she says is true, maybe she has had a hard time tracking you down. You should at least give her a chance; you may like her and find you have loads in common." Annie paused for breath, "if things don't work out, you will always have a home here."

"That's easy for you to say Annie. I don't know if I want to meet her. I'm having a hard time believing she is even alive. Surely someone should have told me she was alive instead of allowing me to believe she was dead all these years. I'm going for a walk, I need time by myself."

As Chelsey let herself out by the back door, Annie sighed and picked up the wedding dress again, her thoughts on Chelsey. She was a troubled girl, who had experienced more in her short life than most people experienced in a lifetime. The last year hadn't been easy but Phil and Annie had come to love Chelsey as their own and Annie suspected that Jason loved Chelsey more than he let on. Maybe he was the one who should talk to her as she thought the world of him.

That evening Jason and Chelsey talked for hours about what she should do. Jason was adamant that she should meet her mum. Chelsey was adamant that she shouldn't. They argued. They calmed down and talked some more.

"Give me one good reason why I should meet her?" Chelsey finally said.

"Because she just might be telling the truth and if you don't go meet her you will be wondering 'what if' for the rest of your life."

"If it was your mum and she wanted to meet you, would you do it?"

"Yes."

The next two weeks changed Chelsey's life forever. She and her mum met up a few times for lunch and they got on great. When it came for Jackie to return to Ireland she invited Chelsey to go with her for a weekend. With the assurance from Annie and Phil that she could return home at any time and with another 'your doing the right thing' talk from Jason and with a great deal of trepidation on her part, she finally agreed.

A few days later Chelsey sat in the guest room of her mum's house in Ireland. She reached for the phone and punched in Annie's number. Jason picked the phone up on the 3rd ring. "Hello"

"Hi Jason, its Chelsey, how are you?"

"Hey, I'm fine, how are things with you? Everything ok?"

"Yeah everything is going well. I've decided to stay for another week. You know, give things a chance and all that."

"That's great; sounds like you two are getting on just fine. Don't forget about us over here will you. Keep in touch."

Chapter One

Five years later...

Strange how memories come flooding back to ones mind. Chelsey looked out of the taxi window at the countryside whizzing past her as she travelled from Liverpool airport towards Anfield. She felt strange coming back here. She leaned her head against the taxi window and thought about the last five years she had spent in Galway city with her mum. She was now part of a real family, no longer an orphan. This made her think about Jason, Phil and Annie. She felt bad as she had lost touch with them. She hoped they hadn't forgotten about her. She wanted so much to see them again. Her thoughts were cut short as the taxi pulled up in front of her grandparent's house. In Ireland her mum lived in a bungalow on its own piece of land and the nearest neighbour lived down the road. She looked up at the two story terraced house in front of her. This would take some getting used to. She paid the taxi driver, opened the gate and walked to the door. Taking a deep breath rang the bell.

Her grandparents turned out to be a lovely couple. Chelsey's Nan, Christine, with her greying brown short curly hair and big square glasses reminded her of the matron that used to run the orphanage. Later Chelsey would get to know just how kind she was. Her granddad, Jack, was a short man, about the same height as Chelsey. He tended to forget things but Chelsey warmed to him immediately.

Christine showed Chelsey up to her room. It was quite big with a double bed and a walk in wardrobe. Beside the bed was a dressing table. A full length mirror was on the wall next to the door. Chelsey sat down on the bed and pulled a photograph of her mum out of her bag. She was sitting on a garden bench wearing a purple sleeveless V-necked top and blue jeans. A heart shaped locket was around her neck. She was laughing. Chelsey wiped the dust off the pine frame on the duvet cover and put the picture on the dressing table. She looked around the room, which was painted cream. The carpet was cream, the duvet cover and the sheets were chocolate brown, the same as the curtains. The furniture was pine. As she admired the decor she pondered on how the two people downstairs that had so long ago told her mother that she couldn't keep her, suddenly wanted to share their home with her. Her mum, Jackie, said they had mellowed a lot and now wanted to get to know their granddaughter. Chelsey hadn't wanted to come but it was important to her mum and after some convincing it became important to Chelsey to get to know her family. She also wanted to find out if she would fit into this place now that she was no longer an orphan or a child living on the streets. The invitation from her estranged grandparents gave her the perfect opportunity to find out.

Chapter Two

Paul Brogan arrived for work at 8a.m. on Monday morning. He was the owner of the clothes shop Brogan Styles. He was early today; the rest of the staff wouldn't start arriving until 8:30a.m. The shop didn't open until 9a.m. Today the replacement girl was starting. One of his sales assistants was on maternity leave. His office was nice and warm due to the early morning June sunshine. It looked like it was going to be another nice day. He took off his jacket and hung it on the back of his chair and had another look at the CV on his desk. Chelsey Ryan already had experience working in a busy shop and by all accounts she was only staying in the UK for a few months. She seemed to be the perfect candidate. He was expecting her at 9a.m.

Jack dropped Chelsey off outside the shopping centre. She looked very business like in her black pin striped skirt, jacket and red blouse. Chelsey got out of the car and pulled a face as she looked up at the building in front of her.

"Brogan Styles in on the second floor." Jack told her, "A Mr Paul Brogan is expecting you."

Chelsey picked up her handbag from the floor of the front seat of the car, "Thanks, I'll see you later."

Jack watched her walk up the steps and disappear inside. He hoped he had done the right thing by finding her this short-term job.

Chelsey walked through the shopping centre and up the stairs to the second floor. She turned left and headed down the corridor. Brogan Styles was one of the biggest shops on the floor. She was ten minutes early but as there were already people inside she went in and asked for Paul Brogan. A blonde haired lady in her 20's showed her to his office. She knocked on the door and went in. A minute later she came out and showed Chelsey in.

"Good morning Ms Ryan," Paul stood and shook her hand.

"Good morning Mr Brogan,"

"Well Ms Ryan you realise that you are here on a temporary basis."

"Yes, I'm only here for 6 months or so."

Looking at her CV again Paul continued, "I see that you have had experience working in a clothes shop before."

"I've been working in a family run clothes shop called Clodagh's for the last five years."

"Good, you can start right away and we'll see how you get on. Now we open at 9a.m but we would expect staff to be here no later than 8:45a.m to set up and sort things out before we open to the public. We close at 5p.m every day except Wednesday and Thursday, we have late night opening till 8p.m. We are closed on Sundays. Here is your work schedule for the month. Make sure you check it carefully as you will be working one late night or a Saturday each week. You will be paid time and a half for that. I'll start you on the minimum wage. Do you have any questions?"

"None that I can think of right now."

"Well if you think of any let me know. I think that is everything." Paul stood up and held out his hand, "Welcome to the team, I'll get Helen to show you the ropes and get you your uniform for today."

Chelsey shook his hand, "Thank you, you won't be disappointed."

Helen turned out to be the girl Chelsey met earlier. She was a couple of inches shorter than Chelsey and had clear blue eyes and long straight blonde hair, which Chelsey was instantly jealous of. She was easy going and immediately put

Chelsey at her ease.

"What did Mr Brogan mean when he said 'you would show me my uniform for today'?" Chelsey asked, following Helen into the changing rooms.

"We wear the clothes we sell in the shop. We change our outfit every couple of days." She explained handing Chelsey a pair of blue jeans and a khaki green print t-shirt. "When you are changed come and find me in the shop and I'll introduce you to the girls and lads and I'll show you the ropes."

For the rest of the day Chelsey got to know the girls and lads in the shop. First there was Helen Adams who was 24. Reece and Anishka Sinclair were sisters. They were 30 and 26 respectively, both outgoing, no qualms about speaking their mind and a great sense of humour. Rebecca Shaw or Becky as she prefers, was the oldest and was the person everyone went to if you had a problem or needed a hand. Lizanne Stevens was the quiet one. She was about 30 and kept herself to herself. She was a hard worker and nobody had any complaints about her. Shauna Roberts was the youngest, only 19. She was always trying new colours for her hair. One day she would be red, the next purple. She liked to be different but she was easy to on with and she was good at her job. Alan Keaney and Dean Williams were the only two male members of the team aside from Paul. They were sales assistants come security guards. Alan at 26 was tall dark and handsome and all the girls who came into the shop loved him. Dean was 25 and was shorter than Alan but just as good looking. Both lads were easy to work with and both had a great sense of humour.

At 5p.m. Jack was waiting for Chelsey outside the shopping centre. "How'd your first day go?" he asked as Chelsey got into his red Ford Escort.

"Better than I expected."

"What did you expect?"

Chelsey turned her head to look out the window. After a moment she shook her head, "I'm not sure." They travelled home in silence. Christine had dinner – chicken curry and rice – on the table when they got home. After saying hello, Chelsey excused herself and went to her room. Ten minutes later she returned dressed in jeans and red three quarter length sleeve t-shirt and cream mules with a red flower on them. She had her short curly brown hair tied up. They started eating and Christine finally broke the silence, "So how did your first day go?"

"Good. Everyone was really nice."

Christine and Jack looked at each other and Jack shrugged. "So did you enjoy it then?" Christine asked.

"Yeah it was ok." After a moment silence Chelsey looked up to find both her grandparents looking at her. She smiled and said, "My day went really well, I enjoyed it. Thanks for getting me the job. Right now I'm just tired."

Christine and Jack sighed with relief and continued to eat. After they had cleared away the dishes they all settled down to watch TV.

By Friday, Chelsey was well settled into her job. It seemed like she had been working there for years never mind a week. She got on well with the staff members and chatted easily to the customers. Friday morning was quiet but by the afternoon things were busy again. Chelsey, Helen and Anishka were working the cash registrars when Paul came out of his office, "Helen you are wanted on the phone, somebody called Sarah." Helen smiled apologetically to a lady who was just about to be served and disappeared into the office.

"Next please," called Chelsey. The lady who was going to go to Helen dumped a basket full of clothes, shoes, bags and belts in front of Chelsey. She started to total them up and continued to talk to Anishka. "So when is your brother getting married then?"

"Tomorrow at 3p.m., if she turns up."

"Is there any reason she won't?"

"Oh Darius is just worried that's all. He's convinced that something dreadful will happen to prevent Stephanie from turning up. He's so nervous and excited and down right terrified at the prospect of getting married that I wonder if he'll be the one who won't turn up." Anishka smiled at the lady she was serving and nodded at the next customer before continuing, "Reece and I are going up their tonight.

"Its great a day off tomorrow," Reece chimed as she arranged shoes on the shelf next to the registrars. At that moment Helen came out of Paul's office looking slightly down.

"Bad news?" Reece asked sympathetically.

"Me and three mates were going out to that new bar opening up tomorrow night and now Sarah is down with an icky stomach so she is going to stay home tomorrow night."

"Ah that's a shame."

"Maybe she will be feeling better by tomorrow night." Chelsey said as she finally smiled goodbye to the lady who had bought half the shop. Helen smiled and went back to serving customers.

"Maybe but I doubt it, Sarah's icky stomachs usually last for a couple of days. Its opening night tomorrow and she was really looking forward to it. Its a shame she is going to miss it" Helen explained as she started tallying up a bright red trouser suit for a girl who was wondering whether to buy red or black shoes to go with it. She obviously couldn't decide as she bought both. Helen turned to Chelsey, "Are you doing anything tomorrow night because you are more than welcome to come, Terri and Louise won't mind."

"Is this the Karaoke Bar that has been advertised all over the place?" Chelsey asked.

"Yeah but its more like an entertainment place with a bar and snacks."

"Sounds like fun, count me in."

Somebody's stomach grumbled and Reece asked, "What time is it?"

"Ten to five," Lizanne replied, she had been so quiet the entire day that the others had nearly forgotten she was there. Alan and Dean started to shut up the shop. Reece yawned which of course immediately set everyone else yawning.

"Sorry," she said, "I'm tired thinking about the drive to Leeds."

"Say congrats to your brother from us." Helen said as the Sinclair girls said goodbye. Paul locked up the shop at five and everyone went their separate ways.

Chapter Three

Saturday morning was dismal but the drizzly rain didn't stop the early morning shoppers. The shop was busy as usual. With only Saturday staff on they seemed busier than usual. They were so stretched that Paul had to work the till just to keep up with the customers. By late afternoon things started to look up. The sun started to shine and the customers began to thin out.

"Well at least it's going to be a nice evening." Helen remarked when she got her first breather for the day. Shauna and Chelsey agreed. "What you doing tonight Shauna?"

"A friend of mine in Kirby just past his driving test so a few of us are going out to celebrate."

Paul, who was putting up 'Mid Season Sale' signs on the two glass doors, looked up suddenly and asked, "Where did Alan go?"

By way of reply Alan walked in laden down with take away, "Grubs up" he said with a grin.

"Yay, food at last." Cheered Shauna.

"You can't eat in here." Paul exclaimed.

"No, but we can eat in your office." Alan responded.

"But it isn't closing time yet."

"Ah come on Paul we didn't even get lunch." Shauna argued.

"Yeah, we haven't had time to breath let alone anything else." Helen put in.

Paul rolled his eyes in defeat. Alan, Shauna and Helen went into Paul's office and left Chelsey and Paul to manage the shop. "Don't worry we will save you some." Alan shouted over his shoulder.

Paul and Chelsey finished putting up the 'Sale' signs and

then enjoyed chicken burger and chips courtesy of Alan while the other three cleaned up the shop. By five o'clock everyone was glad to go home.

At 8:30p.m Helen was waiting for Chelsey in her blue Volkswagen Beetle outside her house. Chelsey said goodbye to her grandparents and got in the car.

"Hiya," said Helen, "you ready?"

"Hi, yep I'm all ready to go."

"I have to go pick up Terri and Louise, they are going to meet us outside the supermarket. It saves me having to go into their street which is a dead end and a pain to get out of. They will probably be late; Terri will be trying on a million and one outfits before she decides which one is right so we will have to just sit tight."

They pulled into the car park but there was no sign of the two girls.

"Speaking of outfits, I love yours." Helen said admiring Chelsey's red linen look knee length skirt and black sparkly sleeveless top. Helen was wearing a baby pink knee length dress and a white coat complete with pink sandals.

"Thanks, you look great yourself." Chelsey beamed. Compliments wasn't something she grew up with and it still made her feel on top of the world when she got one, no matter how small.

Ten minutes later Helen quietly cheered, "Finally here they are."

Chelsey looked up and watched as two girls walked towards the car.

"Terri is the dark haired one and Louise is the red head." Helen explained.

Terri was wearing blue jeans, beige halter neck top and black high healed sandals. Louise was wearing white linen trousers, green top and green shoes.

"Hiya, sorry we're late," Louise apologised as she got in the car, "but Terri couldn't decide what to wear."

"Well I had to be sure." Terri defended herself.

"Girls, this is Chelsey, Chelsey, Terri and Louise." Helen said by way of introduction as she pulled away and headed to the city centre. Helen parked the car and the girls walked through to the bar.

The opening night for the Karaoke Bar was going well, Jason thought as he walked down the street towards the car park where he had left his black Corsa. He heard somebody laughing behind him and looked over his shoulder to see four girls going into the bar. One of them looked really familiar. It was only after they had gone in that he realised who she was. Chelsey Ryan. He never thought she would come back here but there she was as large as life. Jason thought for moment and then turned around and headed for the bar.

By the time the girls arrived it was packed. They went in ordered drinks and found a few empty seats in the corner. The place was quite big. It had a bar in one corner and the stage, which had a karaoke machine to one side of it, was in the other corner. Tables and chairs were set around the walls and there was a dance floor in the middle. The walls were painted red and there were plenty of wall lights to brighten the place up. There were two professional singers, a man and a woman, singing a variety of songs. They were called Kim and Tim Barlow according to the poster outside. They were quite good, Chelsey thought. The owner of the place was trying to encourage someone to get up and sing but as far as the girls could make out he was having no success.

"I wondered if anyone will actually get up and sing and

give that guy a break." Terri had to shout so the other girls could here her over the noise of the crowd and the music.

"Maybe you should when you've had a few drinks." Shouted back Helen.

"Maybe I will."

It took Jason a while to spot Chelsey as the place was so packed. He finally spotted her sitting in the corner laughing with her friends. He was in two minds whether to go and say hello or not. He suddenly felt nervous like it was the first time he had seen her. She looked good, he thought, better than he remembered. More relaxed and with it than the defensive and lonely girl he had known five years ago. He went to the bar and ordered a pint. He looked over at her again and changed his mind. She looked fabulous. Her dark curly hair shone when the light caught it. Her dark eyes shone brightly as she laughed and she had a fascinating smile. He was wondering what to do when the owner, Joe, got up on stage again.

"Which one of you fine people will come up here and give us a song. We don't mind if you're not that good its all for a laugh. Do I have any takers?" When no one moved, Joe tried again but still no one moved. He handed the microphone back to Tim and he started to sing a rock and roll number. This gave Jason an idea and he beckoned Joe over.

After two more songs, Tim and Kim took a break. Joe came back on stage and announced, "Well ladies and gents we have a volunteer to come and entertain us. According to a friend she is really good, so let's give Chelsey Ryan a big hand."

Chelsey who had nearly finished her Gin and Tonic froze in her seat. Everyone started to cheer. She looked around wide eyed at her friends.

"Don't look at me." Helen answered the question in Chelsey's eyes.

Louise laughed and patted her on her shoulder, "Go on,

I'll buy you a drink when you're done."

"Come on Chelsey, don't be shy. I'll give you a free drink for being the first one up." Joe said.

Chelsey finished her drink and stood up. The cheering got louder. When she got on the stage Joe handed her the mike and said in her ear, "Tell Sam there what song you want and I'll get whatever drink you want ready for you."

"I'll have a martini since it's on the house." Chelsey replied and went to the back of the stage to talk to Sam. She decided to sing something upbeat to get the crowd going, not that this crowd needed any encouraging.

Chelsey came back to the front of the stage and suddenly felt very much at home. Singing in front of a crowd was the one and only thing she knew she was good at. During her childhood in the orphanage singing was the only thing that gave her enjoyment. When she did run away, singing was the only thing that stopped her from throwing herself under a bus or off a bridge. While waiting for the music to start, Chelsey thought about the first time she had sang in public. She was fourteen although she wore enough make up to look sixteen. She was in a seedy little bar in London. The owner had wanted someone to entertain as he thought this might distract the men from fighting when they got too drunk to care. Chelsey lied about her age and for about two weeks sang for the patrons. One night two men started a fight and she was hit in the stomach by a stool that had been flung across the room. She spent two days in hospital. It was then she decided to make her way back to Liverpool.

The music started and all Chelsey's worries fell away as she started to sing and dance to the beat. The crowd loved her and sang along. The dance floor was soon full. She was in her element and enjoying every minute of it. Half way through the second verse she saw him. Sitting on his own at the far end of the bar in his black jeans and Liverpool Football shirt, drinking a pint watching her with a grin on his face that stretched from ear to ear. She couldn't believe her eyes. Yet there he was exactly how she remembered him. She almost forgot to keep singing. For the rest of the song her eyes kept straying over to her right just to make sure he was still there and hadn't run off somewhere before she had a chance to say 'hi'. Needless to say he stayed put. He wanted to talk to her just as much as she wanted to talk to him. When she finished the crowned went wild. Applauding, cheering and whistling. She said a quick thank you, ignored the calls for an encore and made a beeline for Jason.

Walking from the stage to the end of the bar a million and one questions went through her head. Did he volunteer her for the song? How'd he know she was here? How mad was he that she hadn't kept in touch? Did he hate her for not coming back to Liverpool sooner, like she had promised? However, she asked none of these. She suddenly felt shy.

"Hi Jason."

"Hi, long time no see."

Joe came over and handed her, her drink, "One martini for one great performance." He was about to say more but Chelsey had reverted her attention back to Jason.

"Sit down, will you." He said, indicating to an empty stool next to him. Chelsey sat down and took a sip of her martini. After a minute silence she looked up at him. They both started to speak at the same time and this caused them to laugh. It broke the ice. Jason put his arm around her shoulders and gave her a squeeze, "It's so good to see you again."

"Did you put me up to that?" Chelsey asked, nodding in the direction of the stage.

"Well this lot looked like they needed livening up. You

seemed like the ideal person to do it." He gave her a cheeky grin. She smiled back.

"I couldn't believe it when I heard my name being called out. Did I sound ok?"

"Would you listen to them?" Jason indicated to the crowd, "They love you. You are even better than I remember. You must have been practicing or something." At this point Joe had finally gotten someone up to sing. A young woman who was wearing a lime green skirt and top was singing in a voice that was as loud as her outfit. "So how have you been?"

Chelsey cupped her hand around her ear, "What?"

He leaned over and said in her ear, "How have you been?"

"Fine." She shouted back, and then she remembered her three friends. She put her hand to her mouth and said, "The girls, I completely forgot about them."

Jason didn't hear what she said but figured she was talking about the girls he had seen her arrive with. As she got up he caught her arm and shouted in her ear, "I'll wait for you outside."

Chelsey went back to the table and the three girls, who hadn't moved, looked at her expectantly.

"You got a fan already?" Louise said

"He's an old friend; I haven't seen him in ages. Listen we're going to get some ice-cream or something. You don't mind do you, I mean me leaving like this, its just that I haven't seen him in a long time." Chelsey trailed off and looked at the three girls. Helen handed her, her handbag with a smile.

"Not at all, enjoy your night."

"Thanks for inviting me out, I've had a great time. I'll see you on Monday." Chelsey turned and headed for the door.

Jason was leaning against the wall when she came out. "Noisy in there isn't it?"

"Yeah, I told the girls we we're going for ice-cream."

"Do you want ice-cream?"

Chelsey shook her head with a laugh. They started to walk towards the car park. Jason broke the silence. "So how have you been?"

She thought about this for a moment, "I've been fine."

"How has it been with your mum?"

"It has taken a while for us to get used to each other but we made it work. It's like we've become a family, which is a dream come true for me. How have you been?"

"Oh, fine."

By this time they had reached the car. Jason unlocked the door. As Chelsey opened the passenger side door, she leaned and arm on the roof and looked across at him. "Fine! That's it? I've been gone five years and nothing new or wonderful has happened to you. No girl-friends to tell me about or any deaths or births or marriages to report."

"No, to all the above." They got in the car and Jason pulled away. "I've moved into a flat with a couple of mates of mine. I'm working in a car repair place in the city centre."

"That explains the oily smell." Chelsey wrinkled her nose, "So Phil and Annie are on their own then. How are they?"

"They're fine." When Chelsey raised an eyebrow, he continued, "Phil is still working as a plasterer and Annie is still dress making. Since I moved out she changed my room into a dress making shop. So now the living room looks like a living room."

"Does she still make wedding dresses?"

"Yeah, every time I call around, she is either just finishing one or just starting a new one."

Chelsey turned and looked out the window, "Where are we going?"

"Don't know, where do want to go?"

Chelsey shrugged her shoulders. She glanced at the clock,

it was ten o'clock. "Shall we go somewhere quiet for a drink?"

"Sounds like a good idea to me. There is a nice quiet pub just around the corner from where I live."

They got themselves drinks and sat talking and catching up on the last five years. At one o' clock Jason dropped Chelsey outside her grandparent's house. Chelsey turned to Jason, "It has been great catching up with you tonight."

"Yeah it has. Listen are you doing anything tomorrow? Phil and Annie would love to see you, they don't go very far on a Sunday we could pop in and say hi."

"I'd love to see them. I'm not doing anything special tomorrow."

"Good, then I'll pick you up after lunch."

"Great, I'll see you tomorrow, well later on today actually," Chelsey pointed to the clock, "it's already Sunday."

She got out the car. Jason watched her as she opened the door and turned and gave him a last wave goodbye. He waved back and drove home.

Chapter Four

Chelsey woke the next morning at nine o'clock. She had never been one for sleeping late. She could hear Christine downstairs. She could also hear the TV so she assumed that Jack was up watching Sky news. She got up and jumped in the shower. When she was dressed in her white skirt and pale green top she went downstairs to get some breakfast.

"Morning darling." Christine called brightly from the sink where she was washing dishes.

"Hi." She sat down to a bowl of cereal followed by jam on toast.

"So how was your night out? Did you have fun?" Christine asked as she poured Chelsey a cup of tea. Between mouthfuls of toast Chelsey related about the night out, meeting up with Jason and how she was going to New Brighton that afternoon to see Phil and Annie.

Jason knocked on Chelsey's door a little after one p.m. The afternoon was turning out to be a nice one. The sun was shining and there wasn't a cloud in the sky. The temperature was in double figures. Chelsey said her goodbyes and got in the car. On the way they talked about everything and nothing but once they got to the other side of the Mersey tunnel Chelsey became very quiet. Jason glanced at her. She was nervous and he knew it. She always went quiet when she was nervous, anxious or upset about something.

"Are you ok?" He asked although he already knew the answer.

"I'm fine."

"Phil and Annie are really looking forward to seeing you. There is nothing to worry about. Just relax." He hoped he sounded reassuring. Chelsey stared at the countryside whizzing past the window and didn't reply. It was like she hadn't even heard him.

Jason pulled up outside 5 Loxham Ave. The house was exactly as Chelsey remembered it. The window boxes were filled with primroses and pansies. The lawn, which was slightly bigger than a postage stamp, was neatly mowed with roses decorating the edges. They even had a white picket fence around the garden. To Chelsey this had been the perfect house and Phil and Annie were the perfect couple.

Annie opened the door when she heard the car pull up. She looked exactly the same. Her dyed blonde hair fell to her shoulders and she had the top of it pulled back in a hair clip like she always did. Her brown eyes lit up as she smiled. All the anxiety that Chelsey felt immediately fell away and she felt like she was at home. Annie ran down the path as Chelsey got out of the car and gave Chelsey a big hug.

"Hi sweetie, it's so good to see you again. It's been too long. You look fantastic. How have you been?"

"Hi Annie, I've been fine, it's so good to be back."

"Well come on into the house both of you. Phil has just gone down to the shop to buy something nice for dinner. He will be back soon."

They all went into the living room and settled down on the sofa. Annie went to the kitchen to organise tea and biscuits for everyone.

"So, Chelsey, tell me what have you been doing with yourself? She asked as she handed tea and biscuits around.

Chelsey took a sip of her tea, "Well I've been working in a clothes shop called Clodagh's for the last few years. It's a family run place and they are all just lovely. I love it there."

"How are things going with your mum?"

"Fine, me and mum get on really well. We have so much in

common. We both like walking and where we live there are so many beautiful country walks to go on. We both like singing and mum is such a good singer. She is great, so encouraging and helpful, I love her to bits." She took another sip of tea and put her cup down on the table. She looked up at Annie and then over at Jason who was leaning against the windowsill. They were both watching her.

"What?" She asked

Annie smiled, "I can't believe you're here, it seems ages ago that you left. When we didn't hear from you I thought we weren't going to see you again. We missed you so much."

"You did?"

"Of course we did."

"I thought you'd be glad to see the back of me. I can't believe you let me stay as long as you did."

Jason laughed and said, "I can't believe Phil let you stay as long as he did. The amount of times he gave you a last chance was unbelievable." Jason came and sat beside her and put an arm around her shoulders.

"Last chances?" Chelsey was puzzled. She looked at Jason and then at Annie. Annie finished her tea and put the cup on the table, she explained,

"Every time you ran away, Phil was going to phone the orphanage to get them to take you back so we didn't have to worry about whether you would come home alive or not."

"So why didn't he?"

"Well me and Jason talked him out of it. Besides he would worry about you wherever you were. The only place he didn't worry was when you were here." They heard the front door open. "That will be him now."

"Hi Annie, I've bought some lamb chops for dinner." Phil called out as he walked in. He opened the living room door which blocked his view of Chelsey and Jason sitting on the sofa. "Where are the kids, Jason's car is..." He trailed off when he turned to close the door and noticed Chelsey. Chelsey slowly smiled.

"Hi Phil."

"Chelsey, I hardly recognised you. How are you luv? Come here and give me a hug."

Chelsey got up and gave him a hug. Phil held her at arms length, "Let me take a good look at you. You've changed so much, I can't get over how grown up you look. You look just great." Chelsey lapped up all the attention.

"You haven't changed a bit." She said, "You're even wearing the same clothes." Phil looked down at his black jeans and bottle green shirt.

"I liked this outfit so much I bought another one exactly the same."

Annie went off to make dinner, roast lamb, roast potatoes and steamed vegetables, polished off with a glass of red wine. When dinner was ready she called everyone in. Even though this was the first time all four had been eating in the same house for the last five years they automatically sat in the same places at the dinner table. It was as if they had never left. They spent the evening talking about old times, laughing at the old jokes and stories. It was after one a.m. when Chelsey and Jason said goodbye. Both Annie and Phil gave Chelsey a big hug.

"You visit again soon. Don't leave it too long. You are more than welcome anytime." Annie said.

"I know I'll be back before you know it. Thank you so much for a lovely evening, I really enjoyed it"

"Are you going to be ok?" Phil asked as she walked down the path to the car. Chelsey turned on her heal and replied,

"I'll be fine. My grandparents don't bite; they are really sweet believe it or not."

Jason opened the driver side door of his car, "see you guys

later" he called. Chelsey waved goodbye and ran down the path as Jason started the engine. She jumped in and waved again as Jason pulled out of the drive.

"Where did Phil think I was sleeping, on the street?" Chelsey asked after a while.

"What do you mean?"

"He asked me if I would be ok." Chelsey raised an eyebrow.

"I told you he worries about you. Ever since you moved he always wondered what you were doing and if you were ok. He was forever asking me if I'd heard from you. He really cares about you despite the fact that you two started world war three most nights."

"Oh!" Chelsey leaned her head back on the seat. She rested her feet on the dashboard and closed her eyes.

"Phil is like that, he worries about everything. It just shows he cares that's all. I'm surprised you hadn't noticed before. You're normally good at noticing those things in people." Not getting any response, Jason glanced to his left but Chelsey was fast asleep.

Chapter Five

Monday morning turned out to be a miserable one. It was overcast with, in Chelsey's opinion, the worst kind of rain, drizzle. Drizzle was deceiving, it looked like you could go out in it and get the things you wanted done, done without getting too wet but once you got home you were soaked. Chelsey got off the bus and walked across the road to work. She couldn't believe she had only been here a week. So much had happened. She climbed the steps toward the front doors of the shopping centre and had to push past two men pasting posters to the glass fronts of the door. Chelsey wondered why they bothered to try and put them up in the rain. The posters were advertising a fashion show for the end of the month. Glancing at her watch she saw it was 9:15 a.m., she was late. Forgetting about the posters she ran up the stairs and down the corridor to Brogan Styles.

"Nice of you to join us Chelsey." Paul greeted her as she walked in.

"Sorry I'm late I had to get the bus in and I missed the first one." Chelsey apologised before going into the changing room and changing out of her red t-shirt into a blue print shirt that Becky had kindly left out for her. As the rest of the girls were in jeans she didn't bother to change her jeans. When she was ready she started to help Reece hang a new shipment of black trousers up at the front of the shop.

"Did you enjoy your weekend?" Reece asked as she opened a second box of trousers.

"Yeah I had a brilliant weekend; I met up with some old friends of mine. It was great to catch up with them. How about you?"

"Me and Anishka were at my brothers wedding in Leeds."

"Of course, the wedding, how did it go?"

"It was a fabulous day. The weather was just perfect. Steph turned up on time, much to Darius relief. She looked fabulous. She wore a two piece dress. White halter neck fitted top, which had sparkly bits all over it and the skirt was really bushy with the same sparkly bits over it. Anishka put the photos in to be developed this morning so they will be done by this afternoon."

Helen came over to the two girls with a box of price tags for the trousers they were hanging up.

"So were did you end up on Saturday night Chelsey?" She asked with a cheeky grin on her face.

Chelsey took the tags and gave her a puzzled look, "What do you mean?"

"Well after you took off with that fella we didn't see you all night."

"What fella?" Reece asked suddenly interested.

"Chelsey met this really cute guy in the Karaoke Bar and he whisked her away. Some people are just born lucky, only here a week and a boyfriend already. So Chelsey who is he?"

Chelsey knelt on the floor, 'born lucky', she thought, if only they knew. She started putting the tags onto the trousers. "He is an old friend of mine that I hadn't seen in a while." Helen raised an eyebrow and glanced knowingly at Reece. She knelt on the floor next to Chelsey and stared to help her. Pushing her blonde hair behind her ear she asked,

"Does this old friend have a name?"

Chelsey looked from Helen to Reece. Both of them were dying to know what had happened and Chelsey knew she wasn't going to get away with saying nothing. She sighed

"His name is Jason."

"And?" Reece prompted

"And nothing, he's a friend, that's all. Since you two are eager to put these on these trousers," Chelsey indicated to the labels on the floor, "I'll go serve some customers." Chelsey got up and walked over to the cash desks and left Helen and Reece to think what they wanted. She felt like everyone in the shop was watching her. As she started to serve the first customer she glanced to her left at Becky who was on the other cash registrar. Becky was arguing with an older lady about the sale price of a cardigan. The lady wanted it for half price even though the label said a third off. Alan and Dean were as usual walking around the shop making sure everything was ok. Lizanne was being her usual quiet helpful self beside the changing rooms at the back of the shop making sure that nobody went in with more clothes than they were allowed. Anishka was sorting a new range of women's sports t-shirts onto hangers. Shauna was re-arranging shoes onto their shelves as some kid had gotten over excited and knocked them all off. Paul was in his office. Chelsey gave the lady she was serving her change and looked at her watch. It was only 10:40 a.m. Lunch wasn't till 12:30 p.m.

By lunch time Chelsey was ready for a change of scenery. Helen and Reece had been giving her the 'I know what you were up to' look all morning. She hated those looks. What did they know about anything? They didn't know her or her friends. She grabbed her jacket and her bag and left to get some lunch and fresh air. She decided to go to the sandwich bar which was around the corner. It had stopped raining and the sun was starting to shine. As she walked towards the sandwich bar she noticed that the two guys who were putting up the posters had successfully managed to stick an orange poster to every shop window and lamppost as far as she could see.

"Just in case you missed one," Chelsey muttered, "as if you

could." She was so deep in thought that she almost collided with a woman coming the other way.

"Oh sorry." She automatically said. The woman nodded and walked on. Chelsey walked on making sure she didn't bump into anyone else.

The queue at the sandwich bar was out the door when she got there. She joined the end and started thinking about what she wanted. She would have chicken, pineapple, lettuce, cucumber and mayonnaise on brown bread. As the queue moved along she came level with the open door and staring her in the face was another one of the orange posters. As she had nothing else to do she read it.

DON'T MISS THE BIGGEST
FASHION EVENT OF THE YEAR
Come join the party as DANIEL RYAN celebrates his 20th anniversary of his famous unique style of fashion.
Back in Liverpool, his home city for the first time in years.
Saturday 29th June, 8:00p.m. The Liner Hotel, Liverpool

Underneath all this was a photo of Daniel Ryan. A man with dark curly hair and big brown eyes and an infectious smile. He looked strangely familiar yet Chelsey couldn't think where she had seen him before. The queue moved again and it was her turn to be served. After she paid for her sandwiches and bottle of water she found an empty bench and sat down to enjoy her lunch. There was another poster on a lamppost across the road from her but it was too far away for her to see it clearly. The photo nagged her. It stirred a long lost memory of someone that she couldn't remember clearly. While she ate she tried to remember who he was. The more she tried the more irritated she became because she couldn't remember. Why did he look so familiar? She never did forget a face. She looked at her watch; 1:15 p.m, her shift started again at 1:30 p.m. She finished her water and then dumped the empty bottle along with the sandwich wrapper in the nearest bin and headed back to work. She tried to forget about the poster but the picture was burned into her memory and she knew she would have no peace of mind until she remembered where she had seen him before.

For the rest of the afternoon that was all she thought about. "Maybe I'm making something out of nothing." She thought. She knew this wasn't true as she never forgot a face. She was so lost in thought that she didn't notice Becky coming up to her. She jumped when Becky tapped her on her shoulder.

"Sorry I didn't mean to make you jump."

"It's alright."

"Are you ok?"

"Yeah I'm fine, why?" She now sounded defensive.

"No reason, you just seemed preoccupied that's all. You didn't look at Reece and Anishka's wedding photos," Becky glanced at the vest tops in Chelsey's hand, "and you're putting size twelve tops on size fourteen hangers." Chelsey looked down at the tops she had hung up.

"Oh, sorry." She started to put them right. Becky saw she wasn't going to get anything else out of Chelsey so went back to the tills.

"Let me know if you need anything." She said over her shoulder.

The time dragged by painfully slow. The shop wasn't particularly busy which was no surprise for a Monday afternoon. By five o'clock Chelsey was tired and hungry. She left without saying goodbye to anyone. She walked over to the bus station and after a short wait got on the bus home. Getting off the bus she noticed that the poster guys had managed to get their posters all over Anfield too. There was one on the lamp-post outside her front door. She rolled her eyes to heaven at it, unlocked the door and let herself in.

Chapter Six

Chelsey went straight to her room and flung her bag on the floor. She picked up the photo of her mum, lay down on her bed and stared at the photo.

"Who is he is mum?" She laughed, "How would you know?"

"Dinner is on the table, going cold." Christine shouted from downstairs. Chelsey swung her legs onto the floor, put the photo back on the dresser and went downstairs for dinner.

"Did you have a good day at work?" Christine asked as she served up fish and chips.

"What? Oh yeah it was ok." Chelsey answered distractedly.

"Are you ok?" Jack asked. Chelsey looked up at him and as her mouth was full of chips she nodded. Christine poured three cups of tea. As she handed them round, Chelsey noticed her long silver necklace which ended in an amber stone. Christine looked down at it.

"You're mum got that for me just before she got married." She said. Chelsey turned back to her half eaten fish and chips when something clicked in her mind.

"Oh course the locket!" She said out loud.

"What locket?" Jack asked. Chelsey ignored the question and jumped up from the table.

"Nan you're a genius." She gave Christine a kiss on the cheek before running out of the dining room and back up stairs to her bedroom. Christine and Jack looked at one another in surprise.

"What was that all about?" Jack asked. Christine shrugged her shoulders.

"Whatever it was it cheered her up."

Up in her room Chelsey sat on the bed looking at the photo of her mum. In the locket around her mum's neck was a photo of her dad. The only one, to Chelsey's knowledge, her mum possessed. She had only seen it once. Her mum wore the locket all the time, even for bed. One day the clasp on the necklace had broken and it fell onto the tiled floor in the kitchen. The locket had opened on impact and the photo inside fell out. The photo was of a smiling young man with curly black hair and big brown eyes. When she inquired of the photo she was told it was her father but he was dead. That was the only time her mum ever spoke of him. Chelsey hadn't thought about it again, until now. It couldn't be the same person, could it? Surely her mum wouldn't lie about her dad, would she? She reflected on her time in the orphanage. Someone had lied about her mum being dead. Nobody ever said anything about her dad. Thinking about it nobody had said much about her mum either until she turned up at the orphanage looking for her. Could her dad be alive? If he was why would her mum say he was dead? Her thoughts were cut short when the phone rang. Jack answered it.

"Chelsey do you want your dinner or not?" Christine shouted from the kitchen. Chelsey realised how hungry she was.

"Yes, I'll be down in a minute" She yelled back. She put the photo back on the dresser and returned downstairs. Christine was about to ask her if she was ok but since she looked more preoccupied than ever Christine turned her attention to Jack who had just come back to the kitchen.

"Who was that?" Christine asked.

"That was Brian Harkin, Peggy had another asthma attack and this time she had to go to hospital." Christine's hand went to her mouth. Jack continued, "Brian was wondering if you wouldn't mind calling in to see her sometime as they are keeping her in for a few days for observation."

"Of course I'll go see her; I'll pop in tomorrow after I do my shopping. Is she in Fazakerley?"

"Yes, ward B room 30." The clock in the living room chimed 6:00 p.m. Jack went back to the living room to watch the news.

"Who is Brian Harkin?" Chelsey asked.

"He is a friend of ours who lives in Bootle. His wife Peggy had bad asthma. She normally keeps it under control with her puffers but sometimes she has a bad attack and it lands her in hospital."

"Will she be ok?"

"Well last time she was in hospital they kept her in for two weeks."

"Is there any more tea going?" Jack shouted from the living room.

"We're out of milk so you will have to have it black or none at all." Christine answered.

"Forget it then."

"You will want some for tonight and tomorrow morning." Chelsey pointed out.

"Are you offering to run up to the shop and get some for us? Christine asked.

"Ok, see you in a bit." As she left the house, the first thing Chelsey saw was the orange poster on the lamppost. This started her thinking about her dad again.

If her dad was alive and well, as the poster seemed to indicate, then why hadn't anyone told her? Why tell her he was dead? Surely her mum would know it he was alive or not and if she knew he was alive why lie about it? It didn't make sense.

What was it her mum had said? He died in a car accident before she was born. That seemed fairly conclusive. So who was the man on the poster? Her dad's brother, cousin or some other long lost relative? What was her dad's name? David? Daniel? Daniel rang a bell. Wasn't that the name of the man on the poster? Chelsey was now at the top of the street. She looked around for a poster but couldn't see one.

"Typical," she muttered, "when you want one you can't see one and when you don't they are staring you in the face."

Reaching the shop she went in and bought the first two litre milk she saw and she headed home again. She stopped and looked at the poster on the lamppost outside her house. Sure enough the man's name was Daniel, Daniel Ryan. She looked up and down the street and seeing nobody she quickly ripped the poster off the lamppost and took it inside.

"Here's your milk Nan." Chelsey said as she put the milk in the fridge.

"Thanks love, what's that?" Christine asked gesturing to the orange paper in Chelsey's left hand.

"Oh this is just an advertisement for a fashion show." She explained briefly and before Christine could say anything else she had left the kitchen and headed back upstairs.

"Thanks for the milk." Christine called after her but Chelsey was too engrossed in the poster to hear her.

In her room Chelsey lay on her bed and scrutinised the poster. She was looking for something, anything that was different to the photo she had seen of her father. After half and hour she was convinced that this Daniel Ryan and the Daniel who was her father were one of the same. That meant he was alive and it also meant that someone had lied to her. She glanced at the photo of her mum. Maybe she should phone her mum and get her to spill the beans. Her mum would only tell her the story she already knew. Who else would know about him? Her grandparents? Yes they would know. Chelsey contemplated how she would go about broaching the subject. After another half an hour of careful thought she headed back downstairs to the living room.

Chapter Seven

Christine and Jack were watching a wildlife program about birds. Christine looked up as Chelsey came in and sat down.

"You ok?" She asked

"Yeah fine." Chelsey watched the TV for a moment before asking, "What happened to my father?" Jack and Christine looked at each other and then at Chelsey. For a moment the only thing that could be heard was the ticking of the clock on the mantelpiece and the narrator talking about how bald eagles look after their young. "Well?" Chelsey prompted. Jack fumbled with the remote and turned the TV off. Christine cleared her throat.

"Honey, you're dad died in a car accident before you were born."

"Mum has told me that story already. What really happened?" Chelsey's tone suggested she wasn't going to leave the subject until she found out the truth.

"But that is what happened." Jack said. Chelsey shook her head. She got up from her seat and walked to the window.

"That's it, he just died. Then why doesn't anyone talk about him eh? Why doesn't anyone have any photos of him? Why is it when I bring up the subject everyone goes quiet like he did something terrible and I'm not supposed to know about it? How did he die?" Chelsey was nearly crying with frustration.

"He died in a car crash about six months before you were born." Christine explained. Chelsey rolled her eyes and looked out onto the quiet street. "Are you sure you want to hear the whole story?"

"Is it that bad?" Chelsey asked sarcastically. Jack got up, went to the kitchen and put the kettle on to make some tea.

They were all going to need it. Christine took a deep breath and began.

"Your mum and dad had only been married for six months when your mum found out she was pregnant. Your dad was out of work and your mum was working as a waitress. They didn't have enough money to buy a house so they lived with us in our old house. They barely had enough money to make ends meet. They couldn't afford a baby. Your mum was on the pill but she had run out of money to buy it after about three months. Your dad had a bit of a temper so she didn't tell him. Jackie knew they couldn't take care of you unless Daniel found a job. For three months she didn't tell him, hoping against hope that he would find work. Eventually she had to tell him. The day she told him, Daniel had just gotten back from an unsuccessful job hunt and he was in a bad mood. The news didn't cheer him up. At first he was shocked. When he found out your mum hadn't been on the pill he got angry. They argued. Dan blamed Jackie for the pregnancy because she didn't take the pill. Jackie blamed him for not being able to take care of you because he couldn't find a job. He stormed out of the house with our car keys. The police called to the house two hours later telling us that our car was in a ditch in Bolton. The car had hit a wall and careened off the road into a ditch. It caught fire and the inside was completely burnt out. The police traced the license plate that's how they found out it was ours. When we got there the body, or what was left of it, was being taken away. Your mum was devastated. She cried for months. We didn't hear from your dad's family again. Jackie lost her job and couldn't support herself let alone a baby. We decided it was for the best that your mum put you up for adoption. They rest you know."

As Christine finished, Jack came in with three cups of tea and biscuits on a tray. He set it down on the coffee table and handed a cup to Christine and one to Chelsey. Chelsey felt like someone had kicked her in the stomach. She sat down on the windowsill and took a sip of tea. It was so hot it stung the back of her throat and made her eyes water. She put the cup on the floor.

"So you two decided to put me in the orphanage." She said quietly. She looked at them both before continuing, "Just answer me one question," She unfolded the poster and put it on the table, "if my dad is supposed to be dead why is his picture plastered on every lamppost and shop window in the city?"

Jack picked up the poster and both he and Christine stared at the face on it. He was older but there was no mistaking who he was. He had even put his name on it. Daniel Ryan was the man who had married their daughter twenty two years ago and had walked out on her. Chelsey didn't wait for a reply. She left the room and the house. Jack and Christine didn't even notice she was gone until they heard the front door slam. Christine jumped up and went to the door. She yanked it open and looked up the street just in time to see Chelsey disappear around the corner. She went back into the living room where Jack was still on the sofa looking at the poster. He looked up as she came in.

"I shouldn't have told her."

"She would have found out one way or another and now that she has seen this," Jack indicated to the poster, "she was bound to want to know what was going on."

"She isn't the only one; I'd also like to know what is going on. How could Daniel be alive? We saw the car it was all smashed up and we saw the body being taken away."

"We saw a body being taken away. We only said it was Dan

because he was the last one to drive it. It obviously wasn't him." Jack threw the poster onto the table.

"If it wasn't him who was it and how could he not tell us he was still alive? He must have known how hard Jackie would take it? She didn't get over him for years." Christine said distraught.

"She also didn't get over you putting Chelsey in the orphanage."

"Oh come on, it was for the best and you know it. Jackie couldn't keep the baby she was broke in more ways than one. She could barely look after herself never mind a baby. You know what state she was in. You said yourself we couldn't look after Chelsey."

"Well you try explaining that to the girl that just walked out of here."

"Oh no, Chelsey," Christine started thinking about her again, "I hope she is ok. Where could she possibly be going? If anything happens to her I'll never forgive myself."

"It will be something else Jackie won't forgive you for."

"I did what was best for our daughter and our granddaughter." Christine snapped, "And stop putting all the blame on me. You agreed to put Chelsey up for adoption." Christine took off her glasses and rubbed her eyes. She was tired. Looking at the clock she saw it was 9:15 p.m. "Where could she have gone Jack?

"Look if we just hang tight she will be back when she has gotten over the shock." Jack said putting an arm around her shoulders. He kissed the top of her head, "I'm sorry for what I said."

"What if she doesn't come back?" Christine looked up at him.

"We will cross that bridge when we come to it."

Chapter Eight

By ten o'clock Chelsey still hadn't returned. It was getting dark and it had started raining. Christine was wearing a hole in the carpet from all her pacing.

"We will have to go and look for her." Christine said finally.

"Look for her where? She could be anywhere."

"Well we can't just stand here and do nothing."

"What about this fella she keeps talking about, the one she met last week? What is his name?" Jack said thinking hard.

"Err, Jason wasn't it?" she said helpfully.

"Yeah, maybe Chelsey has gone to his."

"But we don't know where he lives; we don't know his phone number. I don't even know if he has a phone."

"Well maybe Chelsey has his number written down somewhere. Let's have a look in her room." Jack suggested. They both went upstairs to Chelsey's room. Christine opened the door slowly as if she was opening the door to some sacred place. They both stood in the doorway and looked around the room.

"It will probably be on her dressing table somewhere." Christine whispered. They both went to the dressing table. Whilst Jack sifted through the makeup and skin care products on the dressing table Christine went through the drawers. After about five minutes of searching Christine pulled an orange organiser from the bottom drawer. She opened it to the address book. "Look it will be in here." She set the book down so Jack could look at it. Running her finger down the first page she found nothing. She turned the page and half way down she stopped. "Here it is, Jason." She said triumphantly. Jack took the book downstairs, picked up the phone and dialled the number. It was picked up on the fifth ring.

"Hello?" said a sleepy voice.

"Hello is that Jason? Jack answered, "I'm sorry for ringing you so late. My name is Jack Chislet; I believe you know my granddaughter Chelsey." There was silence for a moment, and then the voice came back,

"Yeah, I know Chelsey."

"Oh good," Jack sounded relieved, "she wouldn't be there with you by any chance would she?"

"No she isn't."

"She isn't." Jack sighed heavily and said to Christine, "he doesn't know where she is." Jason heard Christine sob in the background.

"What's happened?" He asked, although he had an idea. Jack explained what had happened and how Chelsey had stormed out of the house and had been gone for over an hour.

"We thought maybe she had gone to yours. We don't know anywhere else she might go. It's getting late and it's raining and we're worried about her." Jack finished off. Jason thought about this for a moment before saying,

"Look I have a few ideas where she may be, I'll go and see if I can find her."

"Would you? We would really appreciate it." Jack hung up the phone and relayed the message to Christine. Christine collapsed into the nearest chair in relief.

Jason pulled on his coat and picked up his torch, his thoughts on Chelsey. This was just typical of her. She would run away whenever she came up against something she couldn't handle. He supposed it was her way of dealing with it but why she had to choose the nights when it was raining to run off was beyond him. He got into his car and headed toward Stanley Park. Chelsey always ended up somewhere quiet when she was upset. He remembered the first time she ran away from Phil and Annie's. She was only fifteen. Jason had been trying to convince Phil to allow Chelsey to stay. Phil had wanted to ring the orphanage and have her taken back. This led to an argument. Chelsey listened to the whole thing from the kitchen. She left by the backdoor and ran off without telling anyone. When Jason realised she had gone he left to look for her. By the time they found her Jason had convinced Phil, Annie and about half a dozen policemen to help him. She was found four hours later on the beach sitting on a rock looking out to sea. It took Jason another two hours to convince her to come home. It had been raining that night too. They had both come down with rotten colds after that. He sincerely hoped it wouldn't take six hours to get her home tonight. Jason's watch read 10:30p.m when he arrived at Stanley Park. He got out the car and pulled the collar of his jacket up against the steady drizzle. He turned on his torch and walked into the park. By the time he got to the kids play area he was about to give up and try somewhere else when he spotted a lonely figure sitting hunched over on the roundabout.

Chelsey was sitting on the roundabout with her arms wrapped around her legs trying to keep warm. She had walked out without a coat so her jeans and shirt were soaked. She looked up when she saw the light of the torch.

"I thought I might find you here." Jason said.

"Jason? What are you doing here?" Chelsey looked up at him, shielding her eyes from the light. Jason sat down next to her and rested the torch on his lap.

"Your grandparents phoned asking if you were at mine. They are really worried about you."

"Yeah right!" Chelsey said sarcastically.

"Well your Nan started crying when I said you weren't."

"You're lying, I don't believe you." She accused.

"Why would I lie?"

"Same reason everyone else does." She retorted angrily.

"Who's everyone?"

"My grandparents, my mum, my dad." Chelsey wrapped her arms tighter around her legs in an effort to keep the cold from chilling her to the bone.

"Look its cold out here. Why don't we get in the car and go back to my place. We can talk about this there where it is dry and warm." Jason said getting up.

"I'm fine here." Chelsey racked her wet hair behind her ears.

"You're soaking wet, you'll catch a cold if you stay out here in the rain." Jason was starting to get impatient. He always got impatient with her when she was like this. She glared up at him almost daring him to leave her. He sighed, "Chelsey please I don't want to stand out here all night."

"Well go home then, I didn't ask you to come looking for me. I'm a big girl I can look after myself; I've been doing it since I could walk."

"You're right you didn't ask me to look for you, I volunteered and do you want to know why? Because I care and there are two people waiting for you at home who also care about you. I've never lied to you and I'm not lying now." He was loosing his temper now. He wondered why he put himself through it each time but in his heart he knew he couldn't rest knowing she was out here alone. Chelsey got to her feet and struggled to get the words out,

"Care about me! They don't care about me they never have. They are the ones that put me in the stinking bug infested place they call an orphanage. So don't you tell me they care about me Jay because you don't know anything." She sounded hysterical.

"Look I don't know what happened between you and your grandparents or between you and any other member of your family for that matter but I do know when someone is worried and your grandparents are really worried about you." Jason wiped his forehead with the back of his hand. When he got no reply he said in a quieter tone, "can we please get out of the rain. Come back to my place and we can sort it out there." He turned around and headed for the car. Chelsey muttered something under her breath and followed him.

They didn't speak until they pulled up outside Jason's flat. Jason parked the car, got out and unlocked the door. Chelsey followed him inside. They climbed the stairs to the second floor and stopped outside number four. Jason unlocked the door and held the door open for Chelsey. Chelsey looked around the living room. It was small with a two-seater sofa pushed against the wall. An easy chair was pushed against the opposite wall. There was TV in the far corner, with a stereo system on a shelf above. The carpet was a dark brown and in need of hovering. The windows were covered with heavy brown curtains that looked like they hadn't seen the inside of a washing machine in a long time. Beside the sofa was a small table, which was covered with newspapers, TV guides and coffee stains. Jason picked up the papers and his jacket that were adorning the sofa.

"Sorry about the mess, I wasn't expecting company."

"Don't worry about it." Chelsey said still looking around. Jason disappeared down the hall. Chelsey went to the kitchen which was smaller than the living room. The floor was covered in black and white tiles. The sink, which was under the only other window in the room, was full of dirty dishes. Chelsey guessed they had been there a few days. The bin was nearing overflowing point. The kitchen looked in need of a good clean which didn't surprise her as she had never seen Jason actually clean anything. "Typical bachelor pad" she thought.

She looked down the hallway. The bathroom was on her left. There was a closed door to the right, one next to the bathroom and one at the end of the hallway. She went back to the living room and sat on the sofa.

Jason came out of his room in a dry set of clothes. He was carrying another pair of navy tracksuit bottoms, a shirt and towel. "I thought you might like some dry clothes," he said handing them to her, "they are the smallest ones I have. Use my room, first on the right." He walked into the kitchen giving her no time to object. "Would you like a drink?" He called over his shoulder.

"Sure." She replied before going into his room to change. His bedroom was much the same as the rest of flat, messy and in need of a good clean. She pulled off her black boots and pulled a face as she realised her socks where soaked too. She pulled them off. She changed into this tracksuit bottoms and shirt. It felt good to be in dry clothes again. They may have been the smallest he had but they were still huge on her. She rolled the sleeves of the shirt up three times so they didn't cover her hands and she tied the shirttails in a knot. She tightened the tracksuit bottoms as tight as she could and rolled the legs up so she could walk without tripping over them. She dried her hair on the towel. She picked up her clothes from the floor and went back to the kitchen.

"Here put your clothes on the radiator." Jason said pointing to the radiator next to the TV. While she was hanging her top to dry Chelsey realised she had come home in that days uniform which meant she had left her own t-shirt at work. That would teach her for running out as soon as five o'clock came. Jason came over and handed her a cup of tea. Chelsey straightened up and took the drink.

"Thank you."

"Don't mention it."

"Where are your flat mates?"

"Mike is visiting his parents in Manchester and Stu works nights as a security guard." Jason picked up his phone from the table and handed it to her. Chelsey looked at his outstretched hand and then looked up at him.

"Call your grandparents." Her expression turned to stone. Her chin went up. "Don't give me that look." He said wearily.

"What look?"

"The 'don't tell me what to do look.'" Chelsey turned away from him. "Just call them, if you don't I will."

"What am I supposed to say?" Chelsey asked with a hint of sarcasm.

"You can tell them you are in Honolulu for all I care, just phone them so they know you're ok." Chelsey took the phone and dialled the number. Jack answered it on the second ring.

"Chelsey is that you?"

"Yeah it's me." The sighs of relief from the other end were audible to Jason.

"We're really sorry for what has happened tonight. We didn't mean to upset you." Jack was about to say more but Christine took the phone.

"Honey we are really sorry. We wanted to tell you earlier but we weren't sure what you knew. We were waiting for the right time and we..." Christine trailed off into silence. When she didn't get a response she pleaded, "Are you ok? Where are you? We are really worried about you." More silence. "Chelsey please talk to me. I'll never forgive myself if anything happened to you."

"I'm fine, I'm at Jason's." Chelsey finally said.

"Thank goodness for that." She relayed the message to Jack. "Look why don't we come and pick you up. You must be tired. We can talk about this in the morning."

"I've got work in the morning."

"Well we can talk about it after you finish work." Christine said encouragingly.

"I have to go now." Chelsey said ending the conversation.

"Ok, we will see you tomorrow. We both love you, you know that don't you?" Christine said realising that Chelsey wasn't coming home.

"You have a funny way of showing it." Chelsey hung up the phone cutting her Nan off. She looked at the phone and was about to throw it on the sofa when she noticed Jason watching her. She placed the phone on the table.

Jason looked at his watch. It read 12:56 a.m. Chelsey was curled up on the sofa. She was tired but she had so many things going through her head, she couldn't sleep. She had retreated into her own world, her own thoughts and was oblivious to her surroundings. She looked exhausted and angry. Her dogged determination to survive, which had been so prevalent in her before she met her mum, had come to the fore again. There was something else in her eyes that Jason couldn't name. Kneeling down in front of her he shook her shoulder and said,

"Why don't you try and get some sleep. You'll feel better in the morning. Whatever happened can be sorted out I'm sure." She shook her head and continued to stare at the floor. Jason sighed; he knew there was no way he was going to get anything out of her. He tried again, "Come on Chels, talk to me, what's going on in you head?" Still no reply. Eventually he said, "I'm going to bed." She didn't move. Jason got to his bedroom door and turned to look at her, "I'll sleep on the sofa and you can have the bed." Still nothing. He went into his room and pulled the duvet off his bed. He came back to the living room and put it over her. She didn't even move when he tucked it in so she wouldn't lose it during the night. If it wasn't for her steady breathing he would have thought she was dead. Jason wanted to say something, but he couldn't think of the right words. Instead he stroked her cheek. Her eyes flittered briefly up to his face and then back to the floor. He went back to his room and closed the door behind him. When the door clicked shut Chelsey stretched out on the sofa. Half and hour later she fell into a fitful sleep.

Chapter Nine

The sun streaming through the kitchen window woke Chelsey up. She sat up and stretched. Looking around the room she tried to remember where she was. When she saw her clothes still on the radiator the events of the night before came flooding back to her. She kicked the duvet off her and swung her legs onto the floor and stood up. She wondered what the time was so she looked around for clock but couldn't see one. Walking to the window she looked outside. Everything was quiet. There was nobody around. The bin men hadn't been out yet. They normally started about seven so Chelsey figured it was about six. She changed back into her own clothes, which were almost dry. She folded the duvet and left it on the sofa along with his clothes. She looked around for her boots but couldn't see them. Standing in the middle of the room she wondered where she had left them. Her gaze was drawn to Jason's bedroom door. She crept to the door and opened it quietly. Her boots were lying on the floor next to his bed. She glanced at him. He had his back to her and he was snoring softly. Chelsey wondered how people who snored didn't wake themselves up. Living with Phil and Annie she had slept in the room next to Jason and his snoring had woken her up more times than she cared to remember. She walked on tiptoe into the room and picked up her boots. She was about to leave when Jason stirred in his sleep and rolled over to face her. She held her breath. The last thing she wanted was for him to wake up. As he rolled over she noticed his watch on his left wrist. She waited a moment to make sure he was still asleep. She leaned over the bed and looked at his watch, 6:24 a.m. She crept back out of the room. She sat on the sofa and pulled her boots on. She stole out of the house and walked down the stairs to the ground floor, unlocked the door and walked out into the early morning sunshine.

She loved this time of the day. Sleeping in bus shelters and the like she looked forward to this part of the day. It was the only time of day when it was quiet and she could forget all her troubles. The early morning sun always warmed her up after the cold night. There was nobody about although she could hear early morning traffic. She could also hear the birds in the trees. She walked around the corner of the block of flats and towards the main road. She could smell the scent of coconut in the air. Looking around she spied a gorse bush growing in the back yard of the flat across the road. Instead of continuing towards the main road she turned right and walked across the road into the yard of the next flat. She loved the smell of coconut. It reminded her of her mum's garden. A huge gorse bush grew at the bottom of the garden and in the summer the garden was always full of the scent of coconut. She plucked the yellow flowers off the bush and ripped them in her hand. Bringing them to her nose she breathed in the delicious aroma and then opened her hand and let the wind blow the gorse across the yard.

Jason woke with a start. He sat up and looked at his watch; it said 6:45a.m. He lay back down. His bedroom door was wide open. He frowned as he tried to think why it was open as he remembered closing it. One name went through his head. Chelsey. He jumped out of bed and pulled on his jeans. He went into the living room with a growing feeling of dread. He stopped short when he saw the empty sofa. "Typical." He said. Going to the bathroom he splashed cold water on his face to wake himself up. He dried his face, his thoughts on Chelsey. He went into the kitchen and poured himself a glass of orange. He glanced out of the kitchen window onto the back yard. He tilted the glass and let the last of the orange pour down his throat. A movement outside caught his eye. He looked outside again to see Chelsey disappear around the corner of the flat across the road. He put the glass on the side and ran to the door. He yanked it open and ran down the stairs two at a time. He yanked the back door open and ran outside. It was only when he was outside he realised he had no shoes on. The gravel cut into the soles of his feet. He walked gingerly onto the road.

"Chelsey" he shouted. She turned around. "Where are you going?" Chelsey looked Jason up and down and started to walk back towards him.

"Nowhere in particular." She said when she was within talking distance of him.

"I was going to make some tea, did you want some?" Since she was hungry she shrugged her shoulders,

"Ok." They went back to the flat.

"You know you shouldn't come out at this time of day with no shoes and shirt on, you're liable to catch cold." She remarked when she noticed him shivering.

"Yeah well I was thinking about you and forgot."

Chelsey was quiet over breakfast which consisted of tea and toast. Jason broke the silence,

"What you thinking about?"

"My dad."

"Your dad?"

"Yeah." Chelsey continued to munch on toast seemingly oblivious to Jason's confusion. She looked at him, "What?"

"Correct me if I'm wrong but isn't your father dead?" Now Chelsey looked confused,

"No, he's alive and well and making millions." Jason still

looked confused. She continued, "but you already knew that so you can drop the confused look."

"I already knew!" He was surprised, "How was I supposed to know that?" Chelsey was reaching for her third slice of toast but his remark stopped her in mid reach. She drew her hand back without any toast and looked across at him.

"How were you supposed to know? You were talking to my grandparents weren't you? I'm sure they told you everything about last night."

Jason shook his head, "they told me they had argued with you and that you had left and they wondered where you had gone." They sat staring at each other across the table, both waiting for the other to speak. When neither spoke, Chelsey reached for the last slice of toast that had now gone cold. Before she took a bite Jason asked, "So what about your dad?"

"My dad is the fella that is head of the biggest fashion show to hit Liverpool in the last twenty years. This fashion show at The Liner Hotel is to celebrate his twentieth anniversary of being a successful designer. He's a millionaire. Or at least that is what the poster said." Jason still looked confused. "Jay you're looking at me like I'm talking double Dutch."

"I'm trying to understand why you would run away. I mean that sounds pretty good to me."

"You don't get it do you." Jason shook his head slowly so Chelsey explained, "He is the reason why I was put up for adoption. My parents couldn't afford a house when they got married let alone a baby. My dad didn't have a job and they lived with my grandparents. The last thing they needed was another mouth to feed. When mum got pregnant he walked out, got in the car and crashed it into a ditch. Everyone thought he was dead, my mum had a nervous breakdown, and my grandparents had no money. They send my mum to Ireland to get better, which she does and my dad somehow

— 56 —

survives and starts making a fortune designing clothes. As for me I'm left at the nearest orphanage to fend for myself." Chelsey rested her chin in the palm of her hand and looked at the half-eaten slice of toast on her plate. She pushed the plate to one side.

"How do you know you dad is this big designer?" Jason asked.

"Without moving her head she looked at him, "I recognised his picture on a poster and Christine and Jack confirmed it was him." She let out a long sigh and stretched. She got up and walked to the other end of the living room. She pushed the curtain back and stood there looking out of the window. It was eight o'clock.

Jason started to clear away the breakfast dishes. "What time are you in work today?"

"I'm not going in."

"Why not?"

"I don't want to."

"That's a good excuse, will it wash with your boss?" She pulled a face. "You've only been here a week, do you want to get the sack already?" Jason looked over his shoulder to where she was standing looking out the window. He looked her up and down before adding, "I'd take a shower first though, you look like death warmed up."

Turning around Chelsey replied sarcastically, "Thanks I love you too."

"I'll get you a towel."

Chapter Ten

An hour later Jason dropped Chelsey at work. She opened the car door to get out. "You will go home this evening won't you; your grandparents are worried sick." Chelsey got out and closed the door. Looking through the open window she said,

"Thanks for breakfast, see you later."

"Chelsey." He caught her attention.

"Jason I will sort it out with my grandparents ok. Stop being a parrot and go to work before you get the sack." She turned around and walked up the steps to the door. Looking at the posters on the glass door she couldn't believe it was only twenty four hours ago when she first saw them. It seemed like an age away.

It was a quiet day at work. The good weather had taken people to the nearest parks and beaches. Chelsey wished she could join them. The time dragged till lunch. After lunch the shop was slightly busier but mostly with window shoppers. Chelsey was clock watching the whole afternoon. She couldn't wait to get out. She was restless. As soon as it was five o'clock she changed form the shop's uniform back into her own clothes, which were still in the changing rooms from the previous day, and was out of the shop before anyone had noticed she was gone. Once outside she headed for the bus station. On her way she stopped to look at one of the posters. She looked at the grinning face of the man who was her father. It was there and then that she made up her mind to find him and confront him. She wanted to know why he had never told his wife he was alive, why he had never looked for her but most of all she wanted to look into the eyes of the man who had deserted her mum and in turn had deserted her.

When Jason arrived home from work at quarter to six he found Chelsey sitting on his doorstep waiting for him. She stood up as he got out of the car.

"What are you doing here? I thought you were going to go home" He said as he unlocked the door. Ignoring the question Chelsey said,

"I want to find my dad."

"Your grandparents will…" Jason trailed off and turned and looked her full in the face, "you want to what?"

"I want to find my dad."

Jason unlocked the door and walked up the stairs with Chelsey en tow. When they got inside the flat he asked, "Do you think that's a good idea?"

"What do you mean?"

He chucked his keys on the table and ran a hand through his hair. The expression on Chelsey's face told him she demanded an explanation. "Well what makes you think your dad wants to be found? I mean he never told your mum or grandparents that he is alive did he? What if he doesn't want to know you? You could be letting yourself in for a disappointment."

"Are you saying I shouldn't find him because I may be disappointed?" Chelsey couldn't believe what she was hearing. "Do you mean to say if you had the opportunity to see your dad you wouldn't?" Her voice raised a pitch. He didn't reply. "No I guess you wouldn't, you have a mum and dad. I've never had a dad, ever. I always thought he was dead and now that I know he isn't, I want to know what it is like to have one. What's so wrong with that?"

"Hey calm down, nothing is wrong with it. I understand that, I'm just saying be careful."

"How could you possible even begin to understand?" She snapped. "You've had a great life."

"I was an orphan as well remember. I've lived on the streets too. I know what its like not to have anyone." Jason started to raise his voice.

"You were an orphan for two years. I was an orphan for seventeen years until my family decided to tell me I wasn't the only Ryan left of the planet. And as for living on the streets you didn't spend more than a week on them. I spent the best part of three years living in bus shelters, tube stations and shop doorways. You have no idea what that's like. And that's not the worst of it. I've been to every back street, flea infested, scum filled place there is. I fought everything and everyone just to stay alive. You want to know why? Because my mum had a nervous breakdown because she thought her husband was dead. My grandparents couldn't afford to keep me. All because one guy couldn't face up to his responsibilities. So I want to make him face up to them now. I want to see the look on his face when I tell him his little scam has been found out." She stopped for breath. "I thought you of all people would understand that, obviously I was wrong." She continued more quietly. She turned and opened the door to leave.

It was at that moment that Jason finally understood why she had come back to Liverpool. She wanted to blame some-one for her past. But she wanted to blame the right person. First she had blamed her mother but then she shifted the blame to her grandparents. Now that she knew the truth about her father she was blaming him and wanted to tell him so she could get on with her life.

"Chelsey," he said quietly, "I'm sorry. I do understand. I want to help." She turned around and looked at him.

"You really mean that?"

Jason nodded.

Forty minutes later Chelsey and Jason were sitting in his living room eating chips and pizza from the take away down the road. Jason was feeling more awake now that he had had a shower and had changed out of his work clothes. Between mouthfuls of pizza Jason asked,

"So how are you going to find your dad?"

Chelsey thought about this for a moment, "Em, I'm not sure; I was hoping you'd help me out with that one."

"Oh right." They finished the chips in silence. The only sound was the radio DJ going on about the breakup of a band Chelsey had never heard of. Jason eyed the last slice of pizza in the box. Chelsey grinned and picked up the box and offered it to him.

"Would you like the last piece of pizza? It's a shame for it to go to waste."

"Well if you insist." He took it and she started to put the empty box and the greasy chip wrappers in the bin.

"You know Jason you really should empty this bin sometime."

"Yeah I know. You should tell your grandparents and your mum about you looking for your dad." He finished the pizza, "I mean they'll be more help finding him than I will considering they know the man. Besides they probably want to get their hands on him as well."

Chelsey emptied the sink of dishes, turned on the tap and waited for the water to warm up. She then filled the sink with water and squeezed the last of the washing up liquid into the sink. The DJ on the radio had stopped talking and was now playing different requests. Jason turned the radio off.

"Hey I was listening to that, put it back on."

"Your grandparents." He reminded her.

"Look I told you I would sort it out with them."

"You said you would do it this evening after work."

"No, you said that not me." She went back to washing the dishes.

"Why don't I drive you over there tonight and you can sort it out and they can help you to find your dad." Jason suggested.

"Are you trying to get rid of me or something?"

"No, I just think you should patch things up with your folks before things get any worse than what they are already, that's all."

"Ok, fine, I'll go over tonight. Now will you please put the radio back on?"

They pulled up outside Chelsey's grandparent's house just after quarter past eight. Jason turned off the engine. He looked across at Chelsey.

"You ready?" He asked.

"Sure." She was trying to appear nonchalant but he knew that she wasn't looking forward to this. Chelsey opened the door and got out.

"Come on the sooner we get this done the better."

Chapter Eleven

Chelsey needn't have worried about a thing. Her grandparents were so delighted that she had finally come home and that she was ok. She was overwhelmed with hugs and kisses.

"Do you want anything to eat darling?" Christine asked as she put the kettle on to make tea.

"No thanks Nan we have eaten."

"Sit down both of you please." Jack said indicating to the sofa. They sat down. Chelsey looked at Jason and he nodded encouragingly. She took a deep breath and said,

"I want to find my dad." She waited for the gasp of surprise that she was sure would come. However, she was pleasantly surprised when Jack calmly replied,

"We figured you might after we saw the poster last night." Chelsey thought about the events of the previous evening. She looked at the floor and said,

"I would like you two to help me. You know more about him than I do." She looked up at them both.

"Did you honestly think we wouldn't want to find him ourselves?" Christine said.

"You mean you will help?" Chelsey looked from Christine to Jack.

"Of course we will help." Christine said and Jack nodded in agreement. Chelsey's face lit up with happiness. She turned to Jason with a big smile.

"See I told you everything would work out." He said giving her shoulders a squeeze. The smile on Chelsey's face faded when she said,

"All I have to do is tell mum."

"Oh don't worry about your mum she will be fine I'm sure." Jack assured her.

"Yeah but its going to be a shock when I tell her that her husband who she thought was dead for the last twenty two years is actually alive." She took a deep breath and got off the sofa, "no time like the present."

Half an hour later she returned to the living room and put the phone back on the stand.

"How is she?" Christine asked, although she wasn't sure if she wanted to know the answer. Chelsey sat back down on the sofa next to Jason.

"Well, she is shocked. She didn't say much, just that she hopes we find him and..." She ended the sentence with a shrug. Everyone was silent trying to imagine what Jackie was going through.

"Is she going to come over?" Jack asked after a little while.

"Yes but she will let us know when she can get time off work and get flights booked."

"So how do you plan on finding him?" Christine asked. Chelsey looked at Jason but as he said nothing she turned to Christine and explained,

"He is going to be here in three weeks time for his fashion show so I'm going to get a ticket and take it from there." The clock on the mantle piece struck ten. Jack yawned, which in turn started everyone else yawning.

"Sorry everyone," he apologised, "but it's been a long day and I'm tired."

"I'd better get going, I've work tomorrow." Jason said getting to his feet. Chelsey got up to show him to the door. He said his goodbyes and shook hands with Jack and Christine. Chelsey followed him to his car.

"So I'll see you tomorrow?" He asked as he unlocked his car.

"Yes, I'll be over to use your laptop to try and buy some tickets online if I can't get tickets from the ticket office or box office or whatever you call it."

She gave him a big hug. After a few moments she let go of him.

"What was that for?"

"Thanks for helping me. You're a great mate." She smiled up at him. He took hold of her hand and gave it a squeeze.

"You know were I am if you need me." He let go of her hand and got in the car. Winding down the window, he asked,

"Are you going to go to the fashion show on your own or did you want to take someone with you?"

"Is that an offer that you'll come with me?"

"If you want me to."

"Jay I don't know if I could do this on my own so I'd ask you to come even if you didn't offer. So yes please I want you to come with me."

"Ok, I'll see you tomorrow." He started the engine and pulled away. Chelsey didn't go back inside the house until he had turned the corner.

The next day at the first opportunity she got, Chelsey phoned the ticket office only to be told that they had sold out within two days. She was given the number for a second ticket office but she got the same reply. All the tickets had sold out. She couldn't believe it. She hoped there were still tickets online that she could buy. She tried to ring Jason but all she got was his voicemail so she left him a message to call her as soon as he could. He rang her that evening.

"Hey, what's the big emergency?"

"I've been phoning the ticket offices and all the tickets have been sold out. So I'm heading over to your place to try on the Net."

"That's fine, I'll pick you up in half an hour, I just want to have a quick shower first, I'm just in from work." Jason replied.

Half an hour later they were sitting in Jason's bedroom waiting for Jason's laptop to start up. When the computer was ready Jason asked, "What is the name of this fashion show?"

"The biggest fashion event of the year. That's what the poster says. Try typing in Daniel Ryan." Jason did and he clicked on 'upcoming shows'. The page that came up gave an overview of all the shows till the end of the year. Jason scrolled down until he found the dates for the Liverpool show and clicked on it. Flashing at the bottom of the screen in the left hand corner were the words, 'ALL TICKETS SOLD OUT'. Chelsey looked at the flashing sign for a moment and then exclaimed,

"What! They only went on sale on Monday, how could they be all sold out?"

"It's a popular show. Everyone who is anyway interested in fashion wants to be at it. Remember he is the biggest name this side of the Atlantic. People from all over Europe are going to be at it."

"Yeah I know that but surely there must be one ticket left somewhere."

"I'll try the ticket web site." The website also turned up nothing. Jason tried every ticket office he could think off. They all came back the same. He even tried e-bay to see if anyone was selling any tickets but this also came up blank. After an hour he stopped looking. He yawned and stretched. Chelsey couldn't believe that every ticket had been sold. All her hopes had been dashed. She felt like her world had come crashing down around her. She was used to things not working out but this was too much to take. She had never wanted anything in her life as much as that ticket. She put her head in her hands. Tears welled up in her eyes and threatened to spill over onto her face. She wiped them away roughly with the back of her hand and suppressed a sob. Jason sat beside her;

he didn't know what to say. There was nothing to say. Chelsey couldn't suppress the sobs anymore. She sobbed quietly as a tear escaped and trickled down her cheek. It was the first time Jason had ever seen her cry and he wasn't quite sure what to do. He put an arm around her and she turned her head and cried into his shirt. For about ten minutes they remained like this, Jason gently stroking her hair while she cried. After a while Chelsey calmed down. Sitting up she roughly wiped her eyes with her hands. When she was in the orphanage she was told not to cry because it didn't help anyone. She was told to buck up and get on with life because nobody wanted a cry baby. Since then she had always put on a brave face, never allowing her emotions to get the better of her. She felt silly for crying now. She felt worse for allowing Jason to see her cry. She stood up and walked out of the room into the bathroom.

She closed the bathroom door behind her and Jason couldn't get her to talk. He didn't know what to do. So he did the only thing he could think of. He picked up the phone and called Annie. When Annie answered he told her the whole story.

"We can't get tickets anywhere, they are all sold out. Chelsey is in a state and I haven't got a clue what to do." Jason finished off. Annie had listened to the entire story without saying a word.

"How badly does she want to go to the show?" She asked.

"You know you said that it would take something major to make Chelsey cry, well she couldn't stop crying when we could find any tickets"

"Wow, that badly." Annie was silent for a moment before continuing, "I've got two tickets for the show and I'm looking for someone to go with. So if she can put up with me for an evening then she is welcome to it."

"Annie you are a star. Chelsey is going to love you for this. I love you mwah. I'll go tell her the good news." He hung up and ran to the bathroom door. He knocked, "Chelsey I've just been talking to Annie and guess what?" No reply. He knocked again. "Chelsey?" Still no reply. A terrible thought went through his head. "You haven't climbed out of the window and shinnied down the drainpipe on me have you?"

"Oh don't be ridiculous." Chelsey snapped. Jason let out his breath in relief.

"Annie has two tickets for the show."

"Good for Annie."

"Well she wants to know if you want to go with her as she has no one to go with." A second later the door opened.

"She does?" Chelsey asked, not quite sure that she heard right. Jason nodded. It took a moment for this information to sink in. Jason had never seen anyone's mood change as quickly as Chelsey's did at that moment. She went from depression to elation in less than a second.

"You mean I can go."

"Yes."

"And I can find my dad."

"Yes." Chelsey let out a cry of pure joy and threw her arms around Jason's neck. Jason hugged her back.

"I have to ring Annie and tell her how unbelievably wonderful she is." Chelsey let go of Jason, picked up his phone and punched in Annie's number.

Chapter Twelve

When Jason met Chelsey for lunch that Saturday she was still grinning like a Cheshire cat.

"I can't believe the show is two weeks today." She said. She took a sip of her coke and added, "I wish you were coming."

"Nah, fashion shows aren't my thing."

"But I'm not going for the fashion show though."

"I know, but still." He took a bite of his doughnut. He chewed thoughtfully for a moment, swallowed and then asked, "What are you going to wear?" From Chelsey's expression he realised that she hadn't actually thought about it so he continued, "It's just that Annie said if you didn't have anything then she could whip you up something on the machine." Chelsey finished her drink.

"I think that's a good idea. I haven't even thought about what I'm going to wear. What do people wear to this kind of thing? I hope Annie has a few ideas."

"When it comes to dresses Annie has plenty ideas." Jason pulled out his phone and scrolled thought his phone book for Annie's number. "She asked me to tell her whenever you had made up your mind." Finding the number he pressed 'call'. He handed the phone to Chelsey, "here you tell her, I have to go to the loo." Jason got up from the table and headed for the toilets.

"Hi Annie, its Chelsey, how are you?"

"Hi sweetie I'm fine thanks and you?"

"Great thanks; Jason just told me that you would make me something to wear for the show if I didn't have something already. Well I don't have anything and I would really appreciate it if you could make me something."

"I thought you might be stuck for something. Of course

I'll make you up something; it won't take long if we keep it simple. You'll have to come over so I can measure you up and we'll get some material and I'll have a dress made quicker than you can say 'Ryan' Fashion Show.'"

"Brilliant, when will I come over?"

"How about tomorrow afternoon, the sooner we start the better."

"Tomorrow sounds great. See you then Annie and thanks."

"Don't mention it, see you soon, bye." Chelsey hung up just as Jason came back to the table.

"Everything sorted?" He asked.

"Yes, Annie is going to make me a dress." She handed him back his phone. "I've a favour to ask, would you drive me over to Annie's tomorrow afternoon please? She needs to measure me up and we need to pick fabric and a pattern."

"Of course, although I think I'll start charging you for taxi fare." He said with a grin.

"Thanks Jay, you're a mate."

The next day Jason picked Chelsey up at half past twelve. She was waiting for him.

"Where have you been, you said you would be here by twelve. I wouldn't mind but you only live around the corner." She scolded him as she got in the car. Jason looked at her and raised an eyebrow,

"And it's nice to see you too." He said with a hint of sarcasm. Chelsey pulled a face,

"Hello, what took you so long?"

"I overslept."

Chelsey rolled her eyes in reply. Less than an hour later they pulled up outside Phil and Annie's house. Phil was mowing the lawn. He turned off the lawn mower and waved to them.

"Annie is in the house waiting for you go on in." He said to Chelsey. Chelsey went up the path and into the house.

"Hi Annie." She called.

"Hi Chelsey come on upstairs, I'm in Jason's old room. The first door on your left at the top of the stairs." The bedroom door opened immediately and in walked Chelsey.

"Yeah, I know, hi." She said with a grin. She looked around the room at the pristine cream walls and she was in awe at the back wall that was decorated in beautiful green, silver and cream wallpaper. "Wow this room looks so much bigger. Did you extend it?" The last time she had been in this room was before she went to Ireland. Then it was filled with Jason's things and the walls were painted a dark blue.

"No we just moved Jason's stuff out and repainted the walls cream. I don't know what took the longest, moving his stuff of repainting." Annie explained.

"How many coats of paint did you need?"

"I think by the third coat the walls looked more cream and less blue." Annie said with a laugh.

"It is just gorgeous, and the canvas is just beautiful," Chelsey said admiring the canvas of white lilies on the wall.

"Thank you, I'm glad you like it. I find it very calming to work in here now. Now let's get you measured for a dress." As Annie got her measuring tape and measure Chelsey up she asked, "What colour do you want?"

"I don't know, something in red or purple or even black will do."

"What kind of red or purple do you like? Dark or bright red, lilac or deep purple?"

"Burgundy is good, or deep purple." Annie wrote down Chelsey's sizes.

"Ok I'll go into town tomorrow and see what I can get in the way of material. What kind of dress do you want?"

"Something I can walk in and not too fussy either. I'm not into too may bows or frills. Some of the dresses we sell are so fussy I think they look awful."

"Well plain and simple suits me too, it will be quicker to make." Annie took down a few magazines from a shelf and handed them to Chelsey. "Have a look through some of these and let me know which style you like. I'm going to make some tea." Chelsey sat down with the magazines and put them on the table. She pulled out the chair and sat down. As she did she glanced out the window. Phil and Jason were still outside and from Phil's gestures she guessed they were having an animated conversation about something. She opened the first magazine and started looking at dresses.

Ten minutes later Annie returned with two mugs of hot tea. "Find anything yet?" She asked as she set the mug next to Chelsey's elbow.

"Thanks Annie, yeah there are a few nice ones in here. I like this one best though." She pushed aside the magazine she was looking at and picked up one off the floor. She opened the page she had marked. "This one." The one she pointed to was halter neck dress that went down longer on one side with a lovely Spanish like frill along the bottom.

"This one isn't too hard to make." Annie said studying it. "Are you sure you want the frill as well?"

"Sure, it looks good in the picture. The top of the dress is quite plain so I don't think it is too fussy."

After they had dinner Jason and Chelsey headed home. "So did you get sorted then?" He asked.

"Yeah, Annie is going to go into town tomorrow and buy some material and then she is going to start making the dress. The one I've picked is absolutely gorgeous; it goes down long on one side and has a cool Spanish frill along the bottom. Sometime next week I'm going to have to go and buy a pair of shoes to go with it." She yawned, "Man I'm tired, I shouldn't be though I haven't been doing anything."

"That's probably why you're so tired." She nodded in agreement. For the rest of the trip Chelsey talked non stop about going to the show and about the dress Annie was making, she was so excited about the whole thing. Jason enjoyed listening to how excited she was. They pulled up outside her house.

"Here you go. See you sometime in the week." Jason said.

"Thanks for taking me. Would you be a darling and take me sometime for my dress fitting please?"

"Of course, anything for you." She got out and walked to the front door. When she reached it she turned and waved goodbye. She went in and after telling her grandparents all what had happened she had an early night.

The Thursday before the show Chelsey left work an hour early. She was on her way to Annie's for a final dress fitting. After telling her work mates her story they had insisted that she go an hour early. They wouldn't hear of her finishing her shift. They were all routing for her. So she left promising that she would take lots of photos, if she was allowed, and she would be back on Monday to tell them how she got on.

Her grandparents and Jason came to see the finished outfit complete with shoes that Chelsey had bought from Brogan Styles that day with the help of the girls in the shop. Chelsey put the dress on upstairs and then came downstairs into the living room so everyone could see her. When she walked into the room everyone was silent as they admired her. Jason was the first to speak.

"Wow! You look great." This summed up everyone's feelings. Chelsey looked at herself in the full length mirror Annie had brought down from upstairs. She looked fabulous. Her dress was burgundy and the fabric shimmered in the light and as she moved. Her sandals were burgundy with a low heal, she didn't dare try walk in anything else.

"You've done a fantastic job Annie, she looks gorgeous." Christine commented as Chelsey continue to admire herself in the mirror.

"You'll be the belle of the ball sweetie." Said Jack.

"Definitely outclass every other girl there." Phil put in.

"Do you really think so?" Chelsey asked looking at them all through the mirror.

"Of course you will," Annie said coming up behind her, "I made the dress, didn't I."

"Annie thank you so much, you're a star." Chelsey gave Annie a hug. Annie hugged her back and then pulled herself away from her embrace.

"I've got some bad news." She said. Chelsey's face fell immediately.

"Don't tell me you can't come on Saturday."

"I'm really sorry honey but I can't. My mum has fallen and put her hip out and she is in hospital. She is coming out tomorrow and I have to go and look after her. My sister is in America and my dad isn't good at looking after people. I've no choice I have to go." Chelsey's shoulders sagged and she looked at the floor. She looked back up at Annie.

"What am I supposed to do? I can't do this on my own." She looked at Annie then at Jason.

"I'll go with you." She turned in surprise to her Nan.

"I didn't think fashion shows were your thing?"

"They usually aren't but then we aren't really going for the show are we. Besides I wouldn't want you to go on your own." Chelsey was too overcome for words. She gave her Nan a big hug.

"Now go upstairs and take that dress off before you ruin it." Christine said. When Chelsey came back downstairs Jack, Christine and Jason were ready to go. Annie covered the dress with a bin liner and gave it to Chelsey.

"Mind you hang this up as soon as you get home. It will be a real pain to iron if it gets too creased. All the best on Saturday. I'll be thinking about you." Annie said as she gave Chelsey another hug.

"See you luv. Don't worry about anything, you're dad is going to love you." Phil said giving her a hug.

"Thanks guys. I'll let you know how I get on." Chelsey waved goodbye and ran down the path and got into the car. When they dropped Jason off outside his house he said,

"Knock them dead on Saturday and if your dad gives you any trouble you tell him to come see me. I'll give you a call on Sunday. Goodnight."

Chapter Thirteen

Jack dropped Chelsey and Christine off at the Liner Hotel at seven p.m. The show wasn't due to start for an hour but they were advised to arrive early. Chelsey handed their tickets to the man at the door and they were shown into the hall. Ushers in the hall told them which table to sit at. They pushed their way through the crowd and found their table, which was to the left of the stage. They both sat down and looked around. The hall was huge. A semi-circle stage had been set up at the back of the hall. The catwalk extended from the middle of the stage to the middle of the hall. On the stage there was an orchestra playing background music.

Tables and chairs filled the rest of the floor space. Each table sat ten people. All the women were dressed in ball gowns and cocktail dresses in every style and colour imaginable. The men were all dressed in their tuxedos. Ushers who were dressed in black suits and pristine white shirts and red waistcoats were showing people to their seats. The security was tight. Bouncers and security guards could be seen standing at the back of the hall near the exits making sure that everything was in order. Chelsey was fascinated with the hall. It was nothing like anywhere she had ever been before. The plush royal blue and gold carpet, the beautiful lights, the gorgeous tables and royal blue and gold chairs and the fabulous round windows in the doors and along the walls that gave it a ship like feel. The tables were laid with beautiful white tablecloths and beautiful hand cut cutlery and crystal champagne glasses. The backdrop to the stage looked like black velvet encrusted with diamonds. It looked like a clear night sky with hundreds of twinkling stars. 'Ryan Fashion' was projected onto the backdrop. Chelsey was so enthralled by it all that she almost forgot why they were there.

Christine was also taking everything in and was trying to be inconspicuous. She felt underdressed in her navy blue skirt and jacket and white blouse complete with matching hat. She reminded herself however, that it was a last minute arrangement and she didn't have a lot of time to think about what to wear. One of the waiters came around to the table and poured a complementary glass of champagne for each of them.

At eight o'clock the lights dimmed and everyone went quiet. The stage and the catwalk were lit up. Onto the stage walked a woman dressed in a full length emerald green sequined dress. Her straight dark brown hair fell to her shoulders and it was swept up on one side with sparkly hair clips. In her hand was a microphone into which she now spoke with a faint cockney accent.

"My name is Amanda Kensington and I'd like to welcome you all to the twentieth fashion show of Ryan fashions. This year is a special year for Mr Ryan. The last time he was here in Liverpool, the place of his birth, advertising his line of fashion was twenty years ago. Since then he has been all over the world and top name shops and stores are fighting to get their hands on his latest styles. Since this is such a historical night Mr Ryan assures me that this will be a night to remember. So now ladies and gentlemen I'm going to hand you over to the man who has made all this possible. Please give a big hand for Mr Daniel Ryan."

Everyone in the audience including Amanda applauded. Chelsey took a sharp intake of breath and gripped the edge of the seat with apprehension and excitement. This was the moment of truth. The moment she had been waiting for. She watched Daniel Ryan her father come on stage and what she saw she couldn't believe.

Daniel Ryan came on the stage dressed in a pristine expensive looking white suit, white shoes complete with black shirt and tie. His brown hair was cut very short. He took the microphone off Amanda and said,

"Thank you Amanda for such a good introduction," he then turned to the audience and continued with a smile, "Isn't she wonderful ladies and gentlemen. Thank you for your warm applause." The crowd continued to applaud.

Chelsey glanced at her Nan who was looking as shocked as she felt. She looked back at the man on stage. She then looked at the wheelchair he was sitting in. She didn't know what she expected but for him to come on stage in a wheelchair was definitely not it. She leaned over to her Nan and whispered in her ear, "Is that him?" Christine nodded slowly. The last time she had seen her son-in-law he was in a rage and he had stormed out of her house and taken her car for a spin. Apart from the wheelchair, the expensive suit and a few grey hairs he looked the same.

On stage Daniel was saying goodbye to Amanda as she walked off stage to the right. He was speaking again but neither Chelsey nor Christine heard what he said. Both of them were trying to figure out why he was in a wheelchair. The answer came to both of them at the same time. They turned to each other and both whispered, "The accident." They both turned back to the stage as Daniel was saying,

"Well I'll stop gabbin' and get off the stage. Please sit back and enjoy the very special show that we have lined up for you tonight." The audience applauded again as Daniel pushed himself off the stage and the first models came on strutting their stuff on the catwalk.

Daniel Ryan's speciality was ball gowns. Practically the entire show was composed of models modelling every possible style of ball gown in every colour of the rainbow. It was fascinating to watch each model walk down the catwalk, do a twirl at the end and then walk back up again. Sometimes the models came down in twos and other times they came down by themselves. It was hard to believe that all these styles, materials and colours for dresses came out of the head of one man.

Intermission was at half past nine. It was at this point that Chelsey began to wonder how she was going to meet Daniel. He hadn't put in another appearance since he opened the show. Chelsey looked behind her and saw a sign for the toilets.

"I'm just going to the loo." She said. She didn't need the toilet but it gave her an excuse to go for a walk. She got up, pick up her bag and headed for the toilets. As she did she looked to her right and saw a brown door leading off to the back of the stage. She looked around her and as no one seemed to be paying any attention to her she veered right and weaved her way through the maze of tables, chairs and people. When she got there she looked around again and saw that nobody had seemed to have noticed her. Looking through the glass window of the door she saw a corridor that took a sharp turn right some ten feet from the door. Nobody was in the corridor so she tried the handle. The door opened. She again looked around her but seeing no one looking her way she gingerly walked through the door and closed it behind her.

Her heart was pounding so hard she was sure that anyone around the corner could hear it. She wiped the palms of her hands on her dress and walked down the corridor trying to make as little noise as possible. The lino on the floor muffled the clip clop of her sandals. When she got to the corner she gave a quick look round it ready to run back into the hall if need be. She saw that the corridor expanded out into a large room. There were steps leading up to the back of the stage in the middle of the room and steps at the far end also leading up onto the stage. She guessed that is were Amanda had gotten onto the stage. She then noticed a ramp next to both sets of stairs and guessed that this was how Daniel had gotten on and off the stage. There was a door at the far end of the stage and she guessed that it led to the dressing rooms. The room itself wasn't big. She could hear the orchestra playing music on stage. It was muffled here beneath the stage and it was also eerily quiet compared to the noise of the hall. She made her way to the far door and again looked through the glass. To the right there was a row of changing cubicles like the ones you would find in a clothes shop. On the left were rows and rows of dresses hanging up. Women were pulling dresses off hangers and handing them over the cubicle doors to the models who in turn changed and handed back the dress they were wearing. These then were hung back up on the racks.

Suddenly a blonde haired lady appeared on the other side of the glass. She looked surprised to see Chelsey there. She waved Chelsey into the room. She then turned away to talk to a dark haired man in a black suit. The man had an earpiece in his ear and a microphone clipped onto his shirt. Chelsey figured he was a security guard. The blonde lady turned back to the window and seeing Chelsey still standing there she opened the door in a business like manner and said to Chelsey,

"Hurry up and get in here you will be on stage in a minute." She caught hold of Chelsey's arm and pulled her into the room. She pulled a short turquoise halter neck dress from the hanger and handed it to Chelsey. She pointed to the cubicle and then turned back to her clipboard. She made a mark on the page and then walked off to the other end of the room to see to some other models. Chelsey looked at the dress in her hand and then looked at the receding back of the blonde lady. She didn't quite know what to do. The blonde lady looked very business like in her black pinstriped suit and her clipboard. She didn't look like a lady to be messed with. Someone tapped her on her shoulder. She turned to see a red haired girl in a fabulous black strapless dress. She said,

"You better hurry up we'll be on soon." Chelsey couldn't see any way out of the situation so she took the dress into the cubicle and changed. The turquoise dress was fitted at the top. The skirt was flared and it came to the knee. It reminded Chelsey of something out of the fifties. She hung the dress Annie had made her on the hanger and stepped out of the changing booth. The blonde lady who was called Justine was waiting for her and took Annie's dress off her and hung it up. She looked down at Chelsey's burgundy sandals and sighed in annoyance.

"Change the shoes and hurry up, we're trying to run a fashion show here." She pointed to the left. Chelsey went in the direction she was shown and found boxes and boxes of shoes stacked up beside the wall. She contemplated on how she would find the shoes that were supposed to go with the dress she had on in the hundreds of shoes stacked against the wall. The red haired girl came up beside her,

"The show can be a bit daunting can't it? I nearly forgot how to match the shoes and dresses myself." With that she turned down the label on the back of Chelsey's dress and said, "You need box number 54."

"Thanks." Chelsey responded gratefully.

"I haven't seen you before at the practice runs, are you standing in for someone?" Chelsey stared at her for a moment wondering whether to confess. It seemed like the ideal way out of the situation. But before she could say anything Justine started calling out numbers and the girl said, "That's me, see you later." She walked towards the door that led to the back of the stage. Chelsey quickly found box 54 and changed her burgundy sandals to the turquoise sandals. She was amazed that they fitted her.

"54." Justine called out. Nobody moved. "Come on ladies which one of you is 54?" It suddenly dawned on Chelsey that it was the numbers of the dresses she was calling out and it was these dresses that were to be modelled on the stage. In dread she realised that she was wearing dress 54. She made her way to the stage door with much trepidation. Before she had time to think of a way out of the situation she was at the start of the catwalk. The stage seemed much bigger now that she was standing on it. The two models in front of her walked down the catwalk. A second later somebody nudged her from behind and a female voice hissed,

"Get a move on you are holding up the show." Chelsey started to walk down the catwalk. She felt like she was walking the plank. Her breathing was shallow and she stared at the back wall. The catwalk felt a million miles long. When she finally got to the end she stopped, not quite sure what to do next. She could hear the clacking sound of healed shoes as the models behind her caught up with her.

"Turn around." Said the same voice. Chelsey turned somewhat disjointedly and started to walk back up the catwalk. As she did she stole a glance to her left and saw the mystified look on her Nan's face. Chelsey gave a nervous smile as their eyes met. When she got to the steps that led down to the back of the stage she was practically pulled back into the changing room and another dress and matching shoes were thrust into her hand. This one was pink. It had feathers around the neckline that made her want to sneeze. It was on her second walk down the catwalk that a problem occurred in the dressing room.

Justine was in charge of making sure that each model got the dress assigned to her and that the sequence of models going down the catwalk was right. All the girls had rehearsed this each night for the last ten weeks so each model knew exactly where she was supposed to be and in which dress she was supposed to be in at any particular time. As the girls filed through the dressing room and out onto the catwalk to strut their stuff one girl was left in the dressing room without a dress to model.

"Come on hurry up and change your dress." Justine told her.

"I would if I had one to change into."

Justine looked down at her clipboard in her hand then back to the girl standing in front of her.

"You're Lisa aren't you?" Lisa nodded. "You're supposed to be in dress 80." Both Justine and Lisa looked for dress 80. The hanger for 80 was there and shoe box number 80 was there but the dress and shoes were gone. Both girls searched the dressing room and the changing cubicles for the dress and the shoes.

"How is it possible that we have lost a dress? This cannot be happening. Not tonight. We've practiced this too much. Where on earth can it be?" She was loosing her cool now. And no wonder. She had sat down and meticulously planned out what each of the twenty models would be wearing. What sequence they would go down the catwalk. Now she was a dress short. She quickly went through her list again and again. Each time the answer was the same. Lisa was supposed to wear dress number 80 on the fourth walk down the catwalk. So where was the dress? The security guard then came over to see what the problem was.

"Alex we are missing a dress." She told him. She ran her finger down the clipboard again willing it to tell her what was wrong.

"A dress is missing? Alex sounded dubious. However when both girls nodded he asked, "Which dress is missing?"

"Number 80." Justine answered shortly. Alex looked

around the room and then said,

"What number is that dress?" Justine followed his gaze to the third changing cubicle. A burgundy halter neck dress was hanging on the door. Justine went to take a closer look.

"This isn't a Ryan dress." She said after examining it.

"What do you mean it's not a Ryan dress?" Alex asked joining her. Lisa who was intrigued also joined them.

"It doesn't have a Ryan label and it isn't numbered? Justine looked up at Alex then Lisa and then back to the dress. Lisa shrugged her shoulders and Alex scratched his head.

"How did it end up in here?" Alex asked perplexed. At this point the models started coming back into the dressing room to change their dresses.

"Thank goodness there is an interval now." Justine said as the girls went to fill plastic cups with water or take a toilet break. Other snacked on bananas and nuts. Justine turned her attention back to the dress. She tapped her pen on the side of the clipboard.

"Ladies, a bit of quiet please." When everyone had quietened down she held up the dress and asked, "Does anyone know where this dress came from? It's not a Ryan dress." Chelsey knew that it was time to own up before anything else went wrong.

Chelsey was standing at the back of the room. In front of her were all the other models and in front of them were Justine and Alex, both of whom were now demanding an answer. She took a deep breath and slowly raised her hand. Justine beckoned her forward. The walk from the back of the room through all the girls to Justine took now more than ten seconds but to Chelsey it felt like ten lifetimes. She felt like a naughty school girl who was now being marched into the principal's office. The eyes of everyone watching her burned into the back of the neck. The feathers around the neck of the dress she was wearing stated to irritate her. They made her want to sneeze but she knew sneezing at this moment would only make matters worse. She couldn't quite figure out why it would make matters worse, she just knew that it would. Standing in front of Justine, Chelsey was an inch shorter than she was. It may have had something to do with the fact that Justine was in three inch stilettos and Chelsey only had kitten heals on. She had little time to think about this as Justine was firing questions at her in quick succession;

"Who are you? How did you get in here? What do you want? Do you realise that this is a restricted area? Chelsey thought the last question was a little unfair as Justine had practically dragged her into the changing room and threw a dress at her and told her to change.

"My name is Chelsey Ryan and as for being here it was you who dragged me in here." Chelsey pointed an accusing finger at the woman. She could also hear a ripple of curiosity and excited whispers go through the girls behind her as she said her name.

"What were you doing back stage to start with; it isn't open to the public." Justine retorted.

"I was looking for somebody."

"Who?" This question was short and Chelsey was taken slightly aback by it. She looked at the stern face of Alex the security guard. She wondered whether or not to tell these people the truth or make something up. She decided to take the plunge because she figured she had nothing to loose.

"I was looking for Daniel Ryan?"

Judging by the gasps and the flurry of more excited whispering that erupted behind her, Chelsey figured that not too many people came looking for Daniel Ryan. Alex now started talking to someone through his microphone, telling them to go and check on Mr Ryan and to double the security around him as the security backstage had been breeched. She thought the woman in front of her was going to faint, for her face turned pale and Chelsey could read disbelief in her eyes. When two more security guards came in to the dressing room she began to realise just how big of a man Daniel Ryan had become. Justine was speaking to her again,

"Why do you want to see Mr Ryan?"

The room went silent at this point as everyone strained to hear her reply. Chelsey wondered what to say. She could tell the truth but she doubted that they would believe her. However, at this moment she couldn't think of a plausible explanation of why she would want to see him.

"Well?" Justine prompted.

Chelsey took a deep breath and looking the woman squarely in the eye, "Because he is my father." The whispering started again. Just then the back stage door opened and in walked Amanda Kensington, the lady who had opened the show. This time she was wearing a gold strapless knee-length dress complete with chiffon wrap. If she was surprised by the scene in front of her she didn't show it.

"Justine," she said, "the final show starts in five." With that she turned and walked out again. A moment later she was on stage giving her final speech. Justine now turned her attention to the models.

"Come on hurry up, you know what dresses to wear and get in position. We've rehearsed this hundreds of times so don't anyone mess up." Girls started running for dresses and shoes. In the amount of time it took Chelsey to turn around the room had gone from as silent as a tomb to so noisy that she couldn't hear herself think. Girls were trying to find shoes that went with their dresses, asking each other what position they were supposed to be in and shouting to there mates to hurry up in the changing rooms. Alex now took hold of Chelsey's arm and she was led through another door at the back of the dressing room, down a hallway and into a small office.

Chapter Fourteen

The office was very plain. It had a bare table in the middle with one chair on this side and two chairs on the other side facing the door. The walls were painted magnolia and the floor was covered in old linoleum. It reminded Chelsey of a police interview room. Alex told her to sit down. She did so.

"When do I get my dress back?" She asked turning to him.

"Just as soon as this mess has been sorted out." Chelsey was somewhat surprised by his American accent. She assumed everyone was English. Reflecting on this she thought if Daniel Ryan was as big as he apparently was then there was no reason why he shouldn't have gotten into America and gotten himself some staff from there. Five minutes later the two security guards she had seen earlier and Justine came into the room. Justine came around the table and sat opposite Chelsey. Alex also came and sat opposite her. The other two guards stood at the door.

"What is your business with Mr Ryan?" Justine asked.

"I told you, he is my father."

"Mr Ryan has no children so maybe you would like to try again."

"Mr Ryan married my mother twenty two years ago and they had a child, me. This happened before he became rich and famous. He also left us which us why nobody here knows about me. I only found out myself a few weeks ago who he is."

Justine and Alex glanced at each other as this information sank in.

"And you expect us to believe you?" Alex asked fixing Chelsey with a penetrating gaze.

"No I didn't think you would believe me. Like I said, I only found out a few weeks ago about Mr Ryan myself. If you want proof, my Nan is in the audience and she will vouch for me. She can positively identify Mr Ryan as the man who married her daughter. I can also get my birth certificate which has his name on it." Chelsey fervently hoped that they wouldn't ask for her birth certificate as she had only just thought about it. She wished she had thought about it before and actually gone to the trouble of getting it.

The room was so quiet for a moment, she could have heard a pin drop. Justine broke the silence

"Give me one good reason why," she indicated to the security guards, "I shouldn't get these guys to kick you out?"

"Because I'm telling the truth and if you don't let me see him now I'll just come back until you do let me see him."

Justine was uncertain about what to do. She looked at Alex who indicated it was up to her. She took a long hard look at Chelsey. For a moment Chelsey thought she was going to be kicked out. However, Justine said, "Excuse me." She got up and left the room.

After what seemed like an age, which in reality was only fifteen minutes, she returned.

"Follow me." She said curtly. Chelsey got up and followed her out of the room. They went back up the hallway, through the dressing room and out the side door that led from the back of the stage to the sitting area. Instead of going left towards the crowd who were now enjoying the grand finale and judging by the applause it was a good one, Justine turned right and headed through another door and up the stairs. At the top of the stairs Justine turned right and went into a room. She indicated for Chelsey to wait in the room while she let herself into another room. A minute later she was back.

"Mr Ryan will see you now." She said indicating to the room she had just come out of. She then left the room and went back downstairs. Chelsey couldn't believe it. Her heart started racing and the blood pumped in her ears. She walked unsteadily toward the door, pushed it open and walked in.

The room was tastefully decorated. There was a beautiful large Italian leather sofa in the living area with a flat screen TV in the corner. The two windows that looked out over the city were draped with red and orange curtains that matched the cushions and the throw on the bed. The carpet was a deep red and the walls were white. Under any other circumstances Chelsey would have admired the decor and come to the conclusion that somebody had paid out a lot of money on this room. As it was Chelsey only noticed the man sitting in a wheelchair at the other end of the room talking to another security guard. He now turned towards her as she closed the door.

"Ah you must be Miss Ryan." He said as he indicated for her to come into the room and take a seat. "Please excuse me if I don't stand," he patted the arm of the chair, "this makes it a little difficult for me." Chelsey nodded as she sat down. "You have caused quite a stir with my staff. My assistant Miss Mackersfield wasn't quite sure what to do with you? How can I help you?"

She was at a loss for words. What could she say, 'well actually you are my father and I want to know where you have been for the last twenty two years' or 'do you remember Jackie Ryan, well I'm her daughter and I'd like to know if you are my father'. She suddenly realised that he was waiting for an answer. She glanced at the man with him.

"Don't worry about Simon, you can say anything in front of him. I have few secrets from my staff."

She finally found her voice, "I wanted to congratulate you personally on such a successful night."

"Thank you, but by all accounts you seemed to have played

a leading role in messing up the proceedings."

Chelsey smiled nervously and replied as light-heartedly as she could, "Well it wasn't entirely my fault, your Miss Mackersfield included me in the proceedings without giving me time to explain."

"Well never mind, alls well that ends well. I had quite a laugh when I saw you going down the catwalk." He looked her up and down, "Although that dress doesn't look so great on you, pink isn't really your colour." Chelsey sighed with relief that he wasn't angry that she had almost ruined his show. She played with the feathers on the dress.

"I did come in a red dress that a friend of mine made but I don't know what happened to it." She said after a moment silence. Daniel wheeled himself over to the mini bar that stood between the two windows.

"Don't worry about it, Justine has enough dresses to worry about, she'll be glad to give you yours back. Would you like a drink?"

"Err, no thanks."

"Not even a Cherry?"

"Well if you're having one."

He poured a Brandy for himself and a Cherry for her.

"So what did you come here for?" He asked as he handed her the drink, "You didn't talk your way through Justine and Alex and my other security guards just to congratulate me on my show." Chelsey took a sip of her drink and set it on the table to the side of the couch she was sitting on.

"I came to talk to you about Jackie Ryan." If Daniel was surprised by this he didn't show it. "Do you remember her?" Daniel drained his glass and set the glass on the table.

"Should I?"

"You married her."

"Did I indeed? Who told you that?"

"Her parents, Jack and Christine Chislet." He said nothing. Chelsey thought she saw fear in his eyes. But it disappeared as quickly as it had come. "Did you marry her?"

"Maybe you've got the wrong Daniel Ryan." He filled his
glass and drank it down. "I mean which woman in her right
mind would marry a cripple like me?" If he was deliber-
ately trying to avoid the question he was doing a good job.
A little seed of doubt started to form in Chelsey's mind. She
squashed it immediately. After all hadn't her Nan identified
him and besides she recognised him herself from the photo
in her mum's locket. She wasn't sure if he genuinely did not
remember or did he just not want to remember. She searched
his face for an answer but he was giving nothing away.

"You weren't always in a wheelchair. I heard you crashed
your car after you found out Jackie was pregnant with me.
You obviously didn't walk away from it." Chelsey wondered
if she was doing the right thing by telling him what she
knew but she had started now and she couldn't go back.
She continued, "My mum and grandparents thought you
were dead. Mum had a nervous breakdown, she couldn't
look after me and neither could my grandparents so they
put me in an orphanage." She stopped again. She couldn't
believe how calmly she was telling him everything. He still
said nothing. He just sat listening to her. The seed of doubt
surfaced again in her mind. For the first time since seeing
the poster she wondered if she had got it all wrong. What if
she had got the wrong Daniel Ryan? Maybe her grandparents were mistaken. It was over twenty years since they had
last seen him. Even the photo she had seen herself was old
and she had only seen it for a moment. Her Nan had said
they had actually seen the police take a body out of the car
wreck. What if this was all just a horrible coincidence. She
knew how alike total strangers could be. Like the drunk she

had once seen sleeping in the tube stations. She hadn't seen anyone look as scruffy as him. His beard touched the top of his jumper, his clothes were filthy and his shoes were old and cracked. He had an empty bottle of cider beside him. A week later she could have sworn she'd seen him again buying a paper only this time he was looking respectable and as sober as a judge. She was about to apologise for intruding and tell him it was all a mistake when there was a knock at the door. Amanda walked in; she stopped when she saw Chelsey.

"Sorry, I didn't know you had company."

"It's ok Mandy." Turning to Chelsey he said, "Miss Ryan this is Amanda Kensington my niece and right hand woman. Mandy this is Miss Chelsey Ryan; she was just congratulating me on such a good show."

"Hi, nice to meet you, I'm glad you've enjoyed the show." She said extending a hand to Chelsey and giving her a curious look. Chelsey stood up and shook her hand.

"Nice to meet you too."

Amanda turned her attention back to Daniel. "You're wanted on stage for your final speech." Everyone is waiting for you."

"Ok honey I'm on my way." He turned back to Chelsey, "Miss Ryan it was nice meeting you. If you will go with Amanda she will show you to the dressing room and you can get your dress back."

"Thank you." This was all she could muster to say, feeling totally embarrassed by Amanda's intent gaze.

"Follow me." Amanda said and led the way out of the room. Chelsey followed her out and back to the dressing room. When they got there Amanda turned to her and said, "I have to be on stage. You know your way from here don't you?" Chelsey managed a nod before Amanda left her by herself.

Chelsey's mind was in a whirl. She didn't know what to do. She sat on the bench starring at the wall in front of her. How long she sat there she didn't know. She came to when someone tapped her on the shoulder.

"Chelsey, sweetie we have to go." She looked up into the face of her Nan. Christine handed her, her dress and Chelsey took it without saying a word. Five minutes later she walked out of the changing cubicle and dropped the pink dress on the bench. Justine picked it up and hung it on a hanger. Christine handed Chelsey her shoes. She slipped off the pink ones and put on her own. Alex was holding the door open as the girls filed in to change. Christine wrapped an arm around Chelsey and steered her through the models and through the door. As they walked back into the auditorium Christine glanced toward the stage. Daniel was sitting on the stage watching the crowd leave. Christine led Chelsey toward the exit. Daniel watched them leave. Once outside Christine looked for Jack. It was hard to see anything on account of the crowd. They walked down the street and soon spotted him waiting for them on the other side of the road. Chelsey followed Christine to the car and got in the backseat. Christine got in and looked at Jack. She shook her head indicating to him not to say anything.

Chapter Fifteen

Daniel stayed on stage long after the last of the crowd had left.

"Dan," A voice behind him broke through his thoughts. He turned to see Amanda walking towards him. "Are you ok?"

"What? Oh, yes I'm fine." He said distractedly.

"Are you ready to head to the bar for something to drink before we go to our rooms? Justine and Alex and the girls have already gone. The rest of the security guards are dong the final check and are going to head there too soon." Amanda came closer to her uncle. He was starring again at the exit door. "Dan?" He shook his head and finally said,

"I'll be right there Mandy, go and wait for me in the bar." She stayed for a moment trying to figure out what was wrong but she gave up, turned, walked off stage and headed for the hotel's restaurant. Daniel stayed where he was a while longer. He was trying to make sense of what had happened.

He knew Chelsey was his daughter. He had guessed that when Justine had told him about her. When she had walked through the door he knew he had guessed right. She looked so much like Jackie. That was a name he hadn't heard in years. He could still remember every curve of her face. He loved the way she smiled and the way she tilted her head to one side when she was listening to him or concentrating on something. He loved the way the sunlight picked out the red tints in her otherwise dark hair. He had loved her so much. He remembered the day he proposed. They had gone for a walk in Croxteth Country Park. It was a beautiful day and after he had gotten the courage to actually pop the question he couldn't believe it when she said yes. They were married within six months. Things started to go pear shaped soon after the wedding. The company he worked for started laying people off. He was one of the first to go. They then moved in with her parents because they couldn't afford their own place. He couldn't find a job and Jackie's income, as a waitress, was only half of what he used to make. The pressure started to build and it all culminated on that night when Jackie told him she was pregnant. He was furious. They both knew they couldn't afford a child. They both blamed each other. When Jackie's mum joined in the argument on Jackie's side he left the house. Taking Jack's car he drove to the nearest pub. In his haste to get a drink he dropped the car keys on the ground next to the car. Before he had even gotten inside the pub, a drunk picked up the keys got in his car and started the engine. He ran back to stop the man but the man drove over him. The next thing he remembered was waking up in hospital two weeks later. The drunk had driven over his legs and crushed them. He was also suffering from amnesia. By the time he was well enough to leave hospital it was two months later. It took him another ten months to get used to being confined to a wheelchair. He sank into depression. It was only after he accepted his lot that he started to feel better and he started to remember everything about his life. He tried to find Jackie and find out what had happened to her and to his baby but she had disappeared. He sank into depression again and began to think that Jackie wouldn't want him. Not now. Not after he had walked out on her and their child. Now that he was a cripple, she'd never want him. He tried to forget about her but it was impossible. Every day sitting in the wheelchair reminded him of that night and the reason he walked out. Now that reason had turned up demanding answers.

For the last twenty two years he had convinced himself that he no longer needed Jackie and that he definitely didn't need or want a child. Now he couldn't think of anything else.

He berated himself for the way he had treated Chelsey. Why hadn't he just told her the truth? It was obvious that she knew. Why did he avoid the issue and send her away confused and upset? He came back to the only answer there was; he was scared. Scared that if she knew the truth she'd walk away and he'd never see her again. Scared that Jackie wouldn't want him back. Scared that she would have someone new in her life who was treating and loving her the way she deserved. It was only after he had watched Chelsey being led out of the auditorium by Christine that he realised he had probably lost her forever now anyway. He had blown the one and only chance of righting what he saw as the biggest mistake in his life. With this thought he turned, wheeled himself off the stage by way of the ramp and went to meet Amanda who was waiting patiently for him in the bar.

Chapter Sixteen

Once home Chelsey went upstairs to her room.

"What happened?" Jack asked finally. Christine walked into the living room and sat down on the sofa.

"I don't know exactly. She went to the toilet and about two hours later I found her in the dressing room starring at the wall. She was in shock. She only came to when I called her name."

"Has she said anything?"

Christine shook her head. Jack yawned and said, "It's no point worrying about it now. We all need some sleep. She'll be ok in the morning." Christine was unconvinced but she said nothing. As she passed Chelsey's room she pushed open the door. Chelsey was still dressed, lying on her bed with her back to the door.

"Leave her to sleep." Jack whispered.

Christine pulled the door closed and went to bed. She lay awake worrying about Chelsey. She wished she knew what had happened. What was it the American security guard had said?

"Excuse me Mrs Ryan your young friend is in the dressing room backstage. She needs to be taken home."

That was all she had been told. She had followed him back-stage and into the dressing room. A blonde lady had handed her Chelsey's dress and shoes and she had taken Chelsey home. Finally she fell into a fitful sleep.

They both awoke the next morning to the sound of the phone ringing. Jack stretched across and picked up the receiver beside the bed.

"Hello?" He said sleepily. The next moment he was sitting up in bed suddenly wide awake. "Jackie, hiya love how are you?" Christine sat up in bed. She glanced at the clock. It was half past ten. "Chelsey! Err, she's uh, em, well she is..." Christine took the phone off Jack.

"Hiya love, Chelsey isn't good." She quickly explained the events of the night before. "That's all I know." She finished up. "Oh that's great. It will do her the world of good. We'll see you then. Love you. Bye, bye." Christine handed the phone back to Jack.

"How did she take it?" He asked placing the receiver back on the stand.

"She took it very well. She's flying over on Wednesday morning for a week or so." Christine pushed the duvet back and climbed out of bed. "I'll go and tell Chelsey the good news. I hope it does the trick." She left the room and a few seconds later she was back. "She's gone."

"What do you mean she's gone?"

"I mean she's not here."

"Maybe she is downstairs." Christine raced downstairs calling Chelsey's name. Chelsey wasn't in the living room or the kitchen. She looked at the coat rack in the hall and noticed Chelsey's coat was missing.

"Jack" she yelled. Jack appeared at the top of the stairs. "She's not here, her coats gone. Get dressed we've got to go and find her before something happens."

Fifteen minutes later Christine pulled the front door open and headed for the car.

"Chris wait," Jack called, "where are you going to start looking for her. We've no idea where she is."

"Well she is on foot so she can't have gotten very far. Let's just drive around and see if we can see her."

"We don't know how long she has gone. She could be anywhere."

"Could we please stop arguing about it and do something."

Jack grabbed his coat off the rack and was about to pull the front door shut when the phone rang.

"The phone, it may be her now." Jack went back into the house and picked up the phone. Before Christine had reached the door Jack came back out, "That was Jason. We'll pick him up. He says he has an idea were she's gone."

"Head for Stanley Park." Jason said as he got into the back of the car. In no time at all they pulled up beside the park. Jason jumped out and ran towards the children's play area. "Check over there, I'll check the play park." Jason pointed to the bushes and trees over to the right of the park. Aside from a couple of children playing on the swings and a woman who he assumed was their mother he saw nobody else. He went back to the car.

"Find her?" He asked.

Jack and Christine shook their heads. "Did you?" Christine asked hopefully. He shook his head.

"I thought you said she'd be here." Jack's voice rose in frustration.

"I said she might be here." Jason responded.

"Stop arguing about it and let's just find her." Christine said getting back into the car. "Where is she likely to be Jason?"

"She'll be somewhere quiet with few people around. Like a park or a graveyard or something." They pulled out onto the road.

"How about a school playground?" Christine asked pointing to a primary school.

"It's possible."

"But it's locked up; she'll not be able to get in." Jack pointed out.

"If she is upset she'll go out of her way to avoid people.

— 100 —

She'll think nothing of climbing over a locked gate." Jason explained. They stopped and checked the playground. She wasn't here. They drove on and checked every school, grave-yard and field they passed.

"This is ridiculous! She's probably at home wondering where we are." Jack fumed as they turned onto Walton Hall Avenue.

"Isn't that Walton Hall Park down there?" Jason asked pointing to his right.

"What's the likelihood of her being there? It would have taken her ages to get here." Jack said as he pulled over.

"This is Chelsey Ryan we are talking about. It wouldn't surprise me if we found her at Phil and Annie's place." Jason said as he got out of the car. Jack glanced at Christine who shrugged and also got out of the car. She followed Jason. The both walked through the park but saw no sign of her until they turned the corner and went towards the lake. Sure enough there on the other side of the lake sitting on a bench was Chelsey. She was sitting with her heels resting on the edge of the bench and her chin on her knees. She had her arms wrapped around her knees and she was starring into the middle of the lake. Christine and Jason made their way around the lake towards her. Christine was thankful she had the sense to change her dress.

"Hi," Jason said, "May we join you?" Chelsey glanced up at him, then at her Nan and then back to the lake. Christine sat down on the bench next to her and put her hand on Chelsey's shoulder.

"Sweetie are you ok? How long have you been here?"

"It wasn't him." Chelsey said as if she didn't hear her. Both Jason and Christine looked puzzled.

"Who wasn't who?" Christine asked.

"Daniel Ryan, he's not my dad."

"He is. I'd never forget his face."

Chelsey shook her head. "He isn't. We made a mistake. I told him the whole story and he just sat there and looked at me like I was talking the biggest load of nonsense he had ever heard in his life. I'm such an idiot."

"Hey come on, that's hardly fair." Jason said. He sat on the other side of her. "You did what you thought was right, how does that make you an idiot?"

She looked at him and said, "He's dead, he died in the car crash. I just didn't want to believe it because I wanted to blame him so much for everything that happened. Now I've made a complete idiot of myself for practically blaming an innocent man for something he didn't do." Chelsey could feel her eyes welling up with tears. She squeezed her eyes shut willing them to go away. She didn't want to cry. Not for a guy who made a joke about her life. But then she realised she wasn't crying about that, but that he wasn't her father and she so desperately wanted to meet her father and she was never going to be able to do that now. A tear escaped and trickled down her cheek. She wiped it away but she couldn't stop the rest of them.

"It's alright sweetie." Christine put an arm around Chelsey's shoulders and pulled her close, "it's alright."

Chapter Seventeen

It was mid-morning when Daniel Ryan and his associates left Liverpool for London. The mid-day traffic was light but that was nothing unusual for a Sunday morning. The journey gave Daniel a lot of time to think about the night before. He regretted not telling Chelsey the truth. Now it was too late. When they arrived in London he tried to forget about Jackie and Chelsey and focused his mind on sorting out his calendar for the next few weeks. He had two shows in London and then he flew out to Paris for another one.

For the next two days Chelsey went to work, came home and stayed in her room lying on her bed starring at the ceiling. Even the news of her mum coming didn't seem to shake the sombre pall that had come over her. Christine worried that she was depressed. She was no longer upset or angry. She just couldn't be bothered to do anything. She didn't want to listen to the radio or sing or even eat. By the time Wednesday morning came, she hadn't eaten in two days. Her boss told her to take the rest of the week off to get better. Christine wondered whether she should call a doctor. Jack was against the idea.

"Wait till her mum gets here. That will perk her up."

"What time is she landing?" Christine asked. Jack looked at his watch.

"She is landing at eleven. Its quarter past ten now so I'll head off."

"Ok, see you later."

Jackie got off the plane and followed the other passengers into the baggage reclaim. While she was waiting for the baggage to be loaded onto the conveyor belt she thought about the conversation she had with her mum on Sunday.

'Chelsey isn't good.' Her mum didn't know what happened to make Chelsey the way she was. Jackie hoped that it was just a passing phase. Chelsey was a fighter and she usually bounced back. Jackie played with the locket around her neck and her thoughts turned to Daniel. Had Chelsey met him? Was he the same person? Jackie wasn't sure she wanted to know the answer to the last question. It had taken her years to get over his death. When Chelsey phoned her and told her that he was alive, feelings and thoughts that she thought had long been dead and buried rose again. If he was the same person she too wanted to know why he hadn't tried to contact her.

They had only been married for six months. They had talked about having children and they both agreed to wait until they had their own place. So she went on the pill. They could afford it while Daniel had a job but when he lost it; it put a strain on their finances. She mentioned going off the pill to save money but Daniel was having none of it. He said that the pill was a lot cheaper than a baby. Eventually she didn't have money to buy the pill. Then she fell pregnant. Secretly she was thrilled by the news. She had always wanted a baby. It took her ages to pluck up enough courage to tell Daniel. She would never forget that night for as long as she lived. Daniel started ranting and raving about not being told she was off the pill. How he had the right to know what was going on. He blamed her entirely for being pregnant. In a way she supposed it was her fault. Daniel had said she had to give it up because they couldn't give it a decent home. Her head told her he was making sense but in her heart she knew she'd never be able to give it up. When she refused Daniel stormed out of the house taking her parent's car keys with him. Two hours later she was told that he was dead. For the rest of her pregnancy she tried to cope for the baby's sake but once she was born she just fell apart. When she was at work she wondered what was happening to her baby girl. She just wanted to stay at home and look after her. She was the most precious thing in her life. When she stayed at home she didn't have any money. She lost a string of jobs because she took so many days off. She believed she was a bad mother. She was still grieving over the loss of her husband. She became depressed. Eventually she had a nervous breakdown. She was sent to Ireland to recover and her baby girl who was only six months old was sent to an orphanage. It had taken her years to find her again. It was only now that she and Chelsey were getting close, just like a mother and daughter ought to be. Now this has to happen. Just when she thought her life was finally back on track her supposedly dead husband turns up after making his millions. She didn't think she could cope with knowing that he didn't want to be a part of her life. She wasn't convinced he was her husband. She'd seen the car and the burnt body too. It just couldn't be him.

Her train of thought was cut short when the conveyor belt started to move. She grabbed her bags as they went past her and then headed out to the arrivals lounge to find her dad.

"Hiya dad, how are you?" Jackie said giving Jack a big hug.
"Hiya love, I'm ok, how are you?"
"I'm ok, how's Chelsey?" They headed to the car. Jackie placed her bag in the boot of the car and got in the passenger seat.
"Chelsey, I don't know."
Jackie raised an eyebrow and looked at him. "You don't know! What's that supposed to mean?"
"She has stayed in her room for the last two days lying on her bed starring at the ceiling. She won't eat or talk and she doesn't want to do anything. Her boss told her to take the rest of the week off work. She's depressed. We are hoping that

you will bring her out of it." For the rest of the journey they travelled in silence.

Christine met them at the door. "Hiya darling it's so good to see you again." She said giving Jackie a hug.

"Hiya mum, it's great to be back and see you guys again."

Once inside Christine said, "Chelsey is upstairs in her room. The second door on the left."

Jackie left her bags at the bottom of the stairs and went up. She knocked on the door. Getting no response she opened the door. Chelsey was lying on the bed. She raised her head as Jackie opened the door.

"Hiya love."

"Mum." Chelsey suddenly started to cry. Jackie hastened over to her and put her arms around her.

"It's alright honey, I'm here now. Everything is going to be alright." Sobs racked Chelsey's body. Jackie held her tighter. After a while Chelsey calmed down. She pulled away from her mum's embrace and asked,

"May I see the photo?"

Jackie lifted the locket over her head and handed it to her. Chelsey opened the clasp and the picture fell out onto the bed. She picked it up and looked at it. A frown creased her forehead. She leaned over, reached under the bed and pulled out the orange poster. Flattening it on the bed they both examined the two photos.

"That's him isn't it?" Chelsey asked.

Jackie starred at the poster. Her breath caught in her throat and her heart began to beat faster. She put her hand to her mouth and nodded her head as she didn't trust herself to speak. Even though her parents had told her Daniel was alive she didn't believe it until this moment. Ever since she had been told she had thought there must be some mistake. But there was no mistaking the face on the poster. It was Daniel Ryan, her Daniel. The man she had loved and married and who she would have done anything for. The man who fathered her baby. The man who she had thought was dead for the last twenty two years. She didn't understand. If he was alive why hadn't he contacted her? Why had he allowed her to believe he was dead? Didn't he love her?

"I was right all the time, wasn't I?" Chelsey said. "I don't believe it. He sat and made a joke of everything I said. Is he suffering from long term amnesia or something?" It was only when Jackie placed the photo back into her locket that Chelsey realised that she was very quiet. "I'm sorry mum." She said putting her arm around her mum's shoulders. They said nothing for a long time. They sat there on the bed, both finding comfort in each other.

"I can't believe he walked away from that accident and never told me." Jackie finally said, more to herself than to Chelsey. Chelsey was surprised.

"You don't know?"

"Know what?"

"He didn't walk away from the accident. He is in a wheelchair."

It took Jackie a while to digest this piece of information. She finally came to a decision.

"We are going to have to find him and get some answers."

"Mum he has body guards all around him. He has some blondie called Justine who thinks she is part of the Mafia. Besides I already asked him all the questions and he avoided every one of them."

"He may be able to avoid the questions of the daughter he never met but he can't avoid his wife now can he." In answer to Chelsey's puzzled face she pointed to the wedding ring on her finger, "He never divorced me."

Chapter Eighteen

Daniel was sitting in his state of the art apartment in Greenwich. He was trying to think up new designs but his mind was elsewhere. He threw his pencil onto the desk and wheeled himself towards the window. In the street below, people were rushing here and there getting on with their lives. From his vantage point they looked like they hadn't a care in the world. He on the other hand was tormented with thoughts of Jackie and Chelsey. Since meeting Chelsey he had thought of little else. He couldn't get the look on Chelsey's face when he told her to leave, out of his head. She had looked so confused and distraught. She had looked so like her mother. He kept thinking about Jackie. He dreamed about her. He could almost hear her voice. He had to see them both again. He went back to his desk, pressed a button and spoke into the intercom, "Mandy could you come in here for a moment please." A moment later Amanda walked in.

"Yes?"

"Mandy be a love and get me the phone number of a Miss Chelsey Ryan in Liverpool. She is staying at the home of a Mr and Mrs Jack Chislet."

For the next few days Jackie and Chelsey contemplated how to get in touch with Daniel.

"Out best bet I reckon is to catch up with him at his next show." Jackie said as they sat around the table eating breakfast on Friday morning.

"Where is his next show?" Christine asked. Jackie looked at Chelsey. Chelsey shrugged.

"I don't know. Even if we did know and we got there we'd never get a ticket. All his shows are sold out in no time at all."

"Well we can always check." Jackie said pouring herself another cup of tea.

"Suppose so," Chelsey sounded unconvinced, "but I doubt it."

"Are you going to work today?" Jack asked her, changing the subject.

Chelsey looked at him, "Paul's given me the rest of the week off to get better."

"You are a lot better than what you were on Wednesday, so maybe you should go in." Jackie said getting up from the table. Chelsey pulled a face.

"How are we going to find out about his next show?" Chelsey asked.

"I thought your mate Jason had a computer. Can't you look up on the internet and find out?"

"Me! I don't know the first thing about computers."

"I'm sure you could sweet talk Jason into helping you." Christine said, not even trying to suppress a smile. Chelsey got up from the table and ignored the insinuation.

"Well he is at work so it'll have to wait till he gets home this evening."

"In that case you can go to work." Jackie said.

"I don't have to. I have the rest of the week off." Chelsey snapped.

"What are you going to do then? Sit around here watching mindless TV like you have been doing for the last few days?" Jackie inquired patiently, "Your boss thinks your ill and you aren't. Besides it will do you good to have a change of scenery."

"Ok I'll go." Chelsey went upstairs to get dressed.

"That was a bit hard. She has had a shock." Christine said.

"Mum I know Chelsey better than you. She needs to get back to normality even if it is for a few days. Life goes on, shocks or no shocks."

Chapter Nineteen

Everyone at work was so delighted that she was better that they gave Chelsey a huge welcome. It lifted her mood so much. She enjoyed being back more than she thought she would. Friday's were always busy so it didn't seem long before five o'clock came. She walked through the shopping centre with Helen.

"What are you doing this weekend?" Helen asked.

"I'm not sure, what about you?"

Helen shrugged, "Probably go out with the girls, I'm not sure yet." They went down the stairs. "I'm starving, do you want to eat something here or do you have to go home?"

Chelsey looked at the queue at the food court and then looked at her watch. "Nah, I think I'll just go home. Thanks anyway."

"No problem, see you on Monday, I have tomorrow off?"

"So do I, see you on Monday." Chelsey turned to go out of the front entrance when she heard her name being called. She turned to see Jason walking towards her. He looked like he'd just come straight from work.

"Hi." He said.

"Hi, what are you doing here?" Chelsey replied giving him a big smile.

"Giving you a lift home."

"You drove half way across town just to give me a lift home?" They walked out of the centre.

"Yes."

"Why?"

Jason laughed, "Do I need a reason." Chelsey shrugged. "I thought I'd save you a bus fare." They got in the car and Jason pulled away from the kerb. They chatted about their day at work until they passed Chelsey's street.

"Where are we going?" She asked.

"Going to my house. You want to look on the Net for your dad's next show don't you?"

Light dawned on Chelsey. "My mum put you up to this didn't she?"

"Put me up to what?"

"Getting you to pick me up from work. She's feeling bad for making me go to work this morning so to make up for it she gets you to pick me up." Jason said nothing. "I'm right aren't I?" She pressed.

"No this was my idea."

"Then how do you know about me wanting to look on the Net for my dad's next show?"

"Your Nan phoned me and asked if it was ok with me that you use my computer."

"And here's me thinking you actually wanted to pick me up just for the sake of my company." She suddenly felt depressed. Jason glanced at her for a second then at the chip shop up ahead.

"You want fish and chips for dinner?" He asked.

"Sure, whatever."

Chelsey watched him go into the chip shop and thought it was mean of her Nan to ask him to pick her up when he obviously didn't want to. She hated being a burden to anyone and she didn't want him to think that she was some kind of duty he had to fulfil. Jason came back with two portions of fish and chips. Seeing her sullen face he grinned and said,

"If you're interested, it really was my idea to come pick you up." Chelsey turned and searched his face for a moment. He was still smiling and she couldn't help but to smile back.

"Where are your flat mates?" Chelsey asked fifteen minutes later as they sat in Jason's flat eating fish and chips.

"Mike must still be at work. He usually works late on a Friday and I guess Stu is at his girlfriend's place." Jason turned on his computer. "What are we looking for again?" He asked as it started up.

"My dad's next show."

Jason typed in the address and hit the return key. While they were waiting for the web page to come up Jason glanced at Chelsey who was looking at him.

"What?" He asked.

"When did my Nan ring you?"

"About ten minutes before I left work. Why?"

"What did she say?"

"She asked if it would be ok if you came over later on this evening and looked up on the Internet for your dad's next show. I said that it would be fine and I suggested I pick you up. She asked me if I would mind and I said not at all."

A slow smile lit up Chelsey's face as she turned back to the computer screen. Jason scrolled to the bottom of the page and clicked on 'Upcoming Shows'. A list appeared. "There," he said pointing to a date on the screen, "the thirteenth and fourteenth of July in the London Palladium."

"Thirteenth of July, when is that?"

"That's next weekend."

"Are there any tickets left for either show?"

Jason went back to the home page and clicked on tickets. After a moment he said, "No." He looked for a moment longer and then said, "All the tickets have been sold out for the show in Paris too. The next show with available tickets are for the fifth of September and it's in Milan." He looked at her, "You want to go to Milan?" He meant it as a joke but it didn't raise a smile on Chelsey's face.

She sat starring at the computer screen. She felt like some-one had kicked her in the stomach. She couldn't believe it. She clenched her fist and hit the sofa lightly. She felt tears prick the corners of her eyes so she got up and walked to the kitchen without a word. She didn't want to start crying again. She pressed her fingers against her eyes and took a couple of deep breaths until the tears stopped. Jason watched her and his heart went out to her. He didn't think there was anybody to bail her out this time. He shut the computer down and put it away. Chelsey was waiting for him by the front door. She opened it, went downstairs and headed for the car. He watched her go. She looked so deflated that he just wanted to hug her and tell her everything would be fine. But he knew it wouldn't be until she sorted things out with her dad and that didn't look like it was going to happen. He wished he could find Daniel Ryan and make him accept her. He punched the doorframe in frustration. Slamming the door closed he followed her outside.

Chapter Twenty

"What time does Chelsey usually get home from work?" Jackie asked looking at the clock above the mantle piece.

"Usually about half past five, but she has gone over to Jason's to look up dates for Daniel's next show."

From the doorway into the living room, Jackie studied her mum who was sitting on the sofa reading a book. The name Daniel rolled off her tongue like she used it all the time. Jackie on the other hand couldn't even think of the name let alone say it without getting an overwhelming desire to cry. She wasn't sure if she could face him after all these years. She knew she had to if only to answer the list of questions she had. She still loved him but then she thought this was down to the fact that she hadn't fallen in love with anyone else.

Christine looked up from her book, "That's ok isn't it?"

"Sorry?"

"Chelsey going to Jason's."

"Oh, yes its fine."

Christine returned to her book. She looked up a moment later to see Jackie still leaning against the doorframe starring into space. "Are you ok?"

Jackie sighed and came into the room. She sat down on the sofa and shrugged her shoulders. "I don't know if I can face him. But I have to don't I?"

"You don't have to if you don't want to. Nobody is forcing you to."

"Yes I do. I've lived the last twenty two years thinking he was dead and wondering what it would have been like if, well, if things turned out differently. Now I find out he's alive, there are too many questions that I'll be wondering about for the rest of my life if I don't go and see him."

"You still love him don't you?"

Jackie nodded, "What I remember of him, yes." They heard Jason's car pull up outside. A moment later Jack showed Jason and Chelsey into the living room.

"Well?" Christine asked.

"All his shows are booked up until September and it's in Milan." Chelsey flopped down on a chair. Christine looked from Chelsey to Jackie. The both sat with their heads back against their chairs looking deflated upset and tired. Jason thought that he should go but before he got a chance to say goodbye Jack invited him to sit down. He crossed the room and sat beside the window. This was the first time Jackie had laid eyes on him.

'So this was the guy that could do no wrong', she thought. That was the impression she got from Chelsey. She only ever had good things to say about him.

"Jason this is Jackie, Chelsey's mum." Christine said doing the introducing, "Jackie this is Jason."

"Hi, I've heard so much about you. It's nice to meet you finally." Jackie said.

"Hi, nice to meet you too."

"Tea anyone?" Jack asked. When everyone nodded he disappeared into the kitchen. It was while Jack was making a pot of tea that the phone rang.

Chelsey was sitting next to the phone so she answered it. "Hello?" The next instant a look of disbelief spread over her face. "This is who?" Her voice was barely audible. She almost dropped the phone. "It's him." She said. Jackie's mouth fell open and Christine dropped her book on the floor.

"Talk to him." Jason urged. Chelsey looked at him then with a great deal of effort she pulled herself together.

"Daniel, hello, this is Chelsey." She listened for a few

minutes before exclaiming, "You do! But at the show, what was that all about?" She went quiet again. "Yes we can come." Pause. "Mum is here." Another pause. "Tomorrow at ten, fine." She listened for a minute longer before hanging up. She turned to her mum and said, "He wants us to go to London. He's sending a driver up here for ten in the morning to take us down."

Jackie's mouth opened a little wider. "Tomorrow!"

Chelsey nodded.

"Are you sure?" She nodded again.

"He says he is sorry for what he said at the show and he wants to make up for it."

Jackie put her hand over her mouth. "Mum what's wrong?"

"Honey I thought this is what you wanted." Christine said concerned.

Jackie took a deep breath, "It is what I wanted but I didn't think it would be so soon."

Jack came in with a tray of tea and biscuits. "Have a cup of tea and a biscuit and you will feel a bit better." He said. Jackie took the cup of tea offered her and by the time she had finished it the colour was coming back to her face. Chelsey and Jackie looked at each other and simultaneously they thought the same thing. This time they were going to get to the truth. They both grinned.

"I guess we should go and pack." Chelsey said getting up.

"Pack?" Jackie queried.

"He said to bring an overnight bag."

Chapter Twenty One

The next morning everyone was up early. Jack helped Chelsey take their bags downstairs.

"Where is your mum, I haven't seen her all morning." Jack asked

"She is upstairs." Chelsey put her bag on the floor. She went back upstairs and knocked on her mum's bedroom door. Jackie was sitting on the bed still in her dressing gown. "Mum the guy is going to be here in half an hour."

"I don't know what to wear." Jackie got off the bed and walked to the open wardrobe. "I don't know whether to go smart or casual."

Chelsey cast a critical eye over her own outfit, chocolate brown three quarter length trousers, cream top and cream sandals. "Go smart casual." She suggested.

Jackie raised an eyebrow, "that doesn't help."

Chelsey walked over to the wardrobe and surveyed her mum's clothes. After a minute she pulled out a calf-length stonewash denim skirt and a white shirt. "What about this with your white flip flops?" Jackie didn't look convinced. "Mum, wear it, the guy is going to be here soon." On that note Chelsey went back downstairs.

Twenty minutes later a black Mercedes with tinted windows pulled up outside the house. Christine and Chelsey were looking out of the living room window. A heavyset man dressed in a grey suit, white shirt and grey tie got out of the driver's side door. Christine and Chelsey looked at each other.

"I guess he is the driver." Chelsey said as the heavyset man rang the bell.

"I guess so." Said Christine. They both went into the hallway and Christine opened the door.

"Good morning, I'm not sure if I have the right house. I'm here to pick up a Ms Jackie and Chelsey Ryan on behalf of Mr Daniel Ryan."

"Yes you have the right house." Chelsey answered him.

"Oh good, my name is Will. Whenever you are ready we can head off."

"Well my mum isn't quite ready..."

"I'm ready when you are." Jackie said from the top of the stairs. Ten minutes later Jackie and Chelsey said their goodbyes and they set off.

The journey to London was uneventful. When they arrived Will pulled up outside The Tower Hotel. He turned around to them and said,

"Mr Ryan has booked you both a room here. They are booked under the name of Ryan. He has booked a table for three here for seven o'clock." He got out of the car and opened the back door for them to get out. He then got their luggage out of the boot and placed it on the pavement. "Goodbye, enjoy your stay in London."

"Bye Will." Chelsey said.

"Goodbye, thank you." Jackie called after him as he got into the car.

They stood on the pavement looking up at the hotel for a few moments. After seeing a few passersbys giving them funny glances, they picked up their bags and walked into the lobby. They looked around the lobby in awe. Neither of them had ever been in a place like this before. Everything was so expensive and so professionally done right down to the polite 'good afternoon, how can I help you?' they got from the receptionist. Jackie and Chelsey were so taken aback with the impressiveness of the place that they didn't realise the receptionist was talking to them until she repeated,

"Ma'am, can I help you?"

"Oh sorry, yes, err we have rooms booked." Jackie faulted.

"What's the name?"

"Ryan."

"Ah yes two rooms for an indefinite period of time. Your rooms are thirty seven and thirty eight. You will find them on the second floor." The woman then handed two sets of keys to them and waved a porter over. "Rooms thirty seven and thirty eight," she said to the porter, "enjoy your stay."

Their rooms were beautiful. The double bed in the middle of the room was covered with beautiful white bedspread and pillows. The walls were wallpapered with creamy gold wallpaper. The carpet was red. The window was draped in red and creamy gold curtains. There was a coffee table and two comfy cream chairs right by the window so you could drink your coffee and look out at the spectacular view of the Tower Bridge. The en-suite bathroom was the height of luxury. Clean white towels embroidered with 'Tower' hung next to a huge bath. Everything was so clean and polished that Chelsey didn't want to touch anything in case she might spoil the effect. Never in her life had she seen anything like this. And this room was hers for an indefinite period of time. She walked back into the bedroom and sat on the bed. She was so enraptured with the splendour and magnificence of it all that she didn't hear the tap on the door. She came to when she heard her name being called and saw her mum peeping around the door.

"Mum have to ever in your life seen anything like this?"

"I know its amazing isn't it."

"I cannot believe that I spent the best part of four years sleeping on the streets when people live in such luxury."

"I can't believe I'm staying in The Tower Hotel." Jackie sat down on the sofa.

"So what are you going to wear tonight?" Chelsey asked.

"I have no idea. I don't think I have anything fancy enough for dinner at The Tower. At the nearest Chinese maybe but definitely not The Tower." Jackie looked down at her denim skirt, which was now crumpled from the long journey. "I certainly can't go in this." She looked up at Chelsey, "how about you?

Chelsey let out a breath and shrugged her shoulders. "I left my silks and diamonds at home." She said in a mock posh accent." They both laughed. "Seriously I haven't got a clue."

"Well I guess we will just have to dig something out. What time is dinner?"

"Seven."

"What time is it now?"

Chelsey looked at her watch, "Four."

"Good, that gives me enough time to get a shower and decide what to wear." Jackie said getting up and heading to the door.

Chapter Twenty Two

Daniel sat on his bed in front of the mirror knotting his tie. He heard a tap on the door.

"Come in Will."

"Are you ready?" Will asked.

"Yes, just about."

Daniel shrugged on his jacket and looked at himself in the mirror. His black shirt and tie went well with his charcoal suit. He ran a comb through his hair. He looked at Will through the mirror. "Do you think they will come?"

"Of course they will come. They have came this far haven't they?" Will tried to sound cheery.

"What were they like in the car on the way down here?"

"Like I said, they were fine. They talked and laughed about everything. The only time they shut up was when we stopped outside the hotel."

Daniel smiled, "that sounds like Jackie."

"Like mother like daughter."

"Yes. Help me into my chair will you." Will came around the bed and helped Daniel into his wheelchair. "What am I going to say to her Will?"

"Hello would be a good start."

"I haven't seen her in over twenty years and now I'm going to have dinner with her." Daniel started wheeling himself to the door. He continued talking, more to himself than to Will, "Chelsey must hate me. I've been such an idiot."

"Well you can sort all that out tonight." Will encouraged as he walked to the door and opened it for Daniel.

"I hope so."

"Good evening Mr Ryan. You are expected sir." The door-man greeted Daniel as he arrived at the hotel at a quarter to seven.

"Good evening." Daniel wheeled himself into the foyer and was immediately greeted by the receptionist and shown into the restaurant. The head waiter was waiting at the door for him.

"Good evening Mr Ryan, my name is Barry I'll be your waiter for this evening. Your table is ready." Daniel was shown to a table in the far corner of the restaurant beside the window which afforded a splendid view of the river Thames. Barry took away a chair and Daniel pulled his wheelchair into the space provided. Barry then lit the candle in the middle of the table and handed Daniel a menu.

"Thank you." Daniel said.

"May I get you a drink sir?"

"No thank you, I'm waiting on my family to arrive."

"Very good sir." The waiter then left him to himself.

Daniel watched him walk to another table, then looked at his watch. He hoped that Jackie and Chelsey wouldn't stand him up. He played with his gold coloured napkin, which was expertly folded in the shape of a fan. Every few moments he glanced at his watch and then at the door of the restaurant. Twenty minutes later he waved the waiter over.

"Have any messages been left for me?"

"I'll go find out for you Mr Ryan." The young man walked over to the door and spoke with the doorman. A few minutes later he returned to the table, "I'm sorry sir but there are no messages left for you at reception."

"Ok thank you."

"Would you like to order anything sir?"

"No not just yet, thank you."

Daniel glanced at his watch again. It was twenty five past seven. He wondered where the girls could be.

Chelsey came out of her room dressed in a pair of black trousers and a black top complete with red and white print. She walked down the hall to her mum's room. The heals of her black stiletto's made no sound on the carpeted hallway. She knocked gently on the door.

"Come in, the door's open."

Jackie was putting the finishing touches to her make up. "You look great." She said admiring Chelsey's outfit through the mirror.

"Thanks, you are looking fabulous yourself." Chelsey returned the complement.

Jackie was wearing a plain black knee length dress. She tied a black and white print scarf in a knot around her neck to take away from the plainness of her dress. She stood up and walked to the wardrobe and pulled out a pair of black and white heeled shoes. "Do I look too overdressed?" She asked slipping on her shoes.

"You look perfect."

Jackie cast a critical eye over herself in the mirror. She felt nervous. She didn't want to appear over eager, after all this meal might just be a meal but on the other hand she didn't want to look like she hadn't tried. She wasn't sure what she wanted out of this evening. She was hoping it would be more than just a meal.

"Are you sure I look ok?"

"Yes you look great."

"Do you think I should wear the jacket to this dress or..."

"Mum!" Chelsey cut her off, "you look amazing. It will be warm in the restaurant so I don't think you will want the jacket." They looked at each other for a moment. "Shall we?" Chelsey linked arms with Jackie and gestured to the door. Jackie took one last look at herself in the mirror and picked up her handbag.

"Ok, I'm as ready as I'll ever be."

They took the lift down to the ground floor. Walking to the restaurant Chelsey noticed how nervous her mum was. "Everything is going to be fine, just take deep breaths and be calm." Chelsey couldn't believe how calm she felt herself. Jackie took a deep breath as the doorman showed them into the restaurant.

The headwaiter, Barry showed them to their table. The walk from the door to the table took only a few moments but for Jackie it seemed like a lifetime. Her breath caught in her throat when she saw Daniel sitting by the table in his wheelchair. Her step faltered and she felt faint. Chelsey gripped her arm tighter to steady her.

"Come on mum you're doing really well. Only another few steps and you can sit down."

With Chelsey supporting her, Jackie managed to pull herself together and she took the last few steps to her seat. She sat down next to Daniel and Chelsey sat opposite him.

"Hello Jackie." Daniel said.

"Hello Daniel."

"For a minute I was worried that you wouldn't come."

"Well we couldn't very well turn down a meal in The Tower now could we?" Jackie said as light-heartedly as possible.

Daniel gave a nervous laugh and looked down at his hands, "I guess not."

Jackie unfolded her serviette and placed it on her lap. She watched Chelsey do the same. Chelsey felt awkward as the silence extended longer than a minute. She played with her necklace and sighed in relief when Barry came over and asked if they wanted anything to drink.

After ordering Daniel broke the silence, "You look great Jackie."

"Thank you. You are looking well yourself."

The waiter came over with their drinks and took their order for food.

"How have you been Jackie?" Daniel asked after another awkward silence.

"How have I been? I was doing fine up until a few weeks ago. Now I don't know." Jackie faulted, searching for the right words. "I'm having a hard time believing that you are alive. I mean, where have you been for the last twenty two years?"

"I couldn't find you. I tried, you have to believe me."

"You must not have tried very hard."

"I suffered with amnesia for nearly a year after the accident. When I remembered about you and really did look for you but you had gone. I guess your parents had moved too."

"What about your parents and your sister, didn't they think to tell me you were alive?"

"I'm ashamed to say it but they never approved of us getting married so they figured that if you thought I was dead you would move on and start a new life." Daniel hung his head in shame. "I didn't speak to them for a long time after I figured out what had happened. I'm so sorry, I really am."

"For what? For what they did or for what you did?"

"Both. I've regretted that night every day since then."

The waiter came over with their starters and took another order of drinks.

"I don't even know you anymore. I mean you are now a millionaire, head of your own business. You have come a long way from job hunting back in the eighties."

"I still thought of you everyday and wondered what happened to you and to the baby." He glanced across the table at Chelsey.

"It's not a pretty story." Jackie dabbed the corner of her eye with the napkin. She was struggling to keep the tears back.

"I'd still like hear it." Daniel said softly.

Between mouthfuls of sliced melon and roast duck, Jackie poured out her story.

"The night I told you I was pregnant I was hoping against hope that you wouldn't blow your top and that you would be as happy as I was. But you reacted exactly the way I knew you would. I wasn't even surprised when you walked out. I thought you would just drive around for a bit then come back. When the phone rang I knew something awful had happened. When they told us you'd crashed and I saw the mess the car was in, I couldn't cope. It was too much to take. I couldn't bear the thought of living without you.

For the next few months I went about in a daze. I tried to focus on the baby because I wanted her so much. After she was born I fell to pieces. I stayed home most of the time to look after her. I lost a string of jobs. Eventually I couldn't look after myself. I had a nervous breakdown. The only way I could get over it was to get away. I went to Ireland. I told my parents to take care of Chelsea but they couldn't so they put her up for adoption. Living in a new place took some getting used to. It took me years to get over your death. I had to force myself everyday just to get out of bed. I cried myself to sleep every night for so long. When I found out that Chelsea had been given up for adoption I went into the depths of despair. I thought about ending it all so many times but I couldn't do it. I thought that one day I was going to wake up and I'd be fine and I'd go home and find Chelsea and we'd live happily ever after.

By the time I began to feel more like myself it was six years later. I told my mum and dad to find Chelsea. Because of all the laws surrounding adoption and adoption agencies they could only find out so much. She had been moved from the initial orphanage she was put in. When I did go home a few years later Chelsey seemed to have disappeared. I was told she'd ran away and nobody knew where she was. I nearly had another breakdown."

At this point Jackie stopped talking and wiped the tears away from her eyes. She pushed the food around on her plate with her fork. Chelsey reached over and held her hand. Jackie looked at her and saw that she was crying too. Chelsey gave her a small smile which said, 'you're doing great mum, everything is going to be fine.' Jackie took a deep breath and continued her story.

"I read in the paper that a few kids had been caught trying to get a free train ride to London and they had been sent to various foster homes. I hoped against hope that one of them would be Chelsey but she wasn't one of them. Every time I came up against a block I thought about that night you walked out. I knew if you were alive we'd be a family. Because I was always looking for Chelsey I wasn't working so I never had any money. I ended up living off my dad's wages. Sometimes I got so depressed that I didn't eat for days. My mum had to force feed me sometimes.

The first I heard of Chelsey was that she was living in New Brighton. I went across to find her. When I finally did find her she had been befriended by a young man called Jason and his adoptive parents. She agreed to come to Ireland for a weekend. That weekend lasted five years. We got to know each other and over them five years I finally came to terms with your death. I could think about you without crying. I could remember the good times without thinking about that night. She helped me get back on my feet. When she came back here I was pleased for her because I saw it as a way for her to lay to rest all her disappointments and upsets in her life.

When she phoned me and told me you were still alive and she wanted to find you I was sure she had made a mistake.

I thought there had been some kind of misunderstanding and I'd come over and we'd sort out the mistake and have a laugh about it. But then I saw your poster, I didn't know what to think. I couldn't comprehend how you survived and you never told me."

"I'm so sorry." Daniel said quietly.

"So am I." Fresh tears ran down her face. "Excuse me." She got up and headed for the exit. Daniel watched her walk away. He turned to find Chelsey watching him. He had almost forgotten she was there.

"I really am sorry Chelsey. If I could turn the clock back I would."

"I better go and see if she is ok." Chelsey got up from the table.

"Please Chelsey, try and get her to understand that I really am sorry. I don't want to lose her again."

"You will have to give her some time. It will take her a while to get over the shock. But I'll tell her what you said. Thanks for dinner." With that she headed out of the restaurant and upstairs.

Daniel sat for a long time at the table, hoping against hope that they would return. He thought about Jackie's story and felt so bad that she had had a hard time. He couldn't imagine what kind a life Chelsey had had. He was still there at midnight when the restaurant was closing. He came to when he was tapped on the shoulder,

"Excuse me sir," Barry said, "we are closing now." Daniel looked up at the man and then looked around. He was surprised to see that he was the last person in the restaurant. "Would you like me to call a taxi for you sir or call someone to collect you sir?"

Daniel pulled himself together. "No, I'll be fine thank you." He wheeled himself out of the restaurant, pulled out his phone and rang Will. It wasn't long before he was on his way home.

Chapter Twenty Three

Ten o'clock the next morning Chelsey knocked on Jackie's door to see if she was ok and to see if she wanted to go downstairs for breakfast. Jackie was sitting curled up on the sofa in a dressing gown.

"Hi, did you get some sleep last night." Chelsey asked sitting down next to her.

"A little. I've a splitting headache this morning."

"Have you taken something for it?"

"Yes, I've taken a couple of aspirin. I'm just waiting for them to take effect."

"I was thinking of going down for some breakfast. Do you want some? It'll do you some good I'm sure."

"I suppose, I can feel the aspirin starting to work." Jackie got up from the sofa. "I'll get a quick shower."

Twenty minutes later they went downstairs for breakfast. They both just had tea and toast as neither of them were particularly hungry. After a couple of slices of toast, Jackie started to feel a bit better. Over a cup of tea they talked about the night before.

"After you left, Daniel told me that he didn't want to lose you again and that he is really sorry for what happened." Chelsey said.

"Do you think he still loves me?"

"I don't know so much about the whole love thing mum. I guess he must feel something, I mean he did pay for all this." She swept her hand around the room.

"Yeah, I know, but I can't help thinking that he just feels sorry for me and he is trying to make up for it."

"Yeah, but he paid for the room and the meal before he heard your story. Doesn't that count for something?"

"Maybe." Jackie finished her tea and looked outside at the river. She watched the boats of tourists going up and down the river for a while. "I think I'll go for a walk."

"Do you want some company?"

"No I just want to be by myself for a while. Try and sort things out in my head."

After her mum left Chelsey sat in the restaurant and had another cup of tea. She dearly wanted to follow her mum and make sure she was ok but she knew that her mum wanted to be alone so she resisted the urge. She didn't want to stay in the hotel all day so she decided she'd go out for a walk herself. She was looking forward to walking along the river. She reflected on the last time she was in London. She was a scruffy skinny thirteen year old sleeping rough and running away from every uniformed person she came across. She shook her head in disbelief when she thought of how much she had to fight for every mouthful of food she got then and now she just had to call a waiter over and get whatever she wanted and she didn't even have to pay for it. She left the restaurant and headed back to her room for her bag. Five minutes later she was back in the lobby heading for the door.

"Excuse me Miss Ryan."

Chelsey turned at the sound of her name. The girl on reception beckoned her.

"Yes?" Chelsey inquired.

"A Mr Daniel Ryan left a message for you and Mrs Ryan saying that he had called. You also have a visitor." The girl indicated to the seating area on the other side of the lobby. Chelsey looked and couldn't quite believe whom she saw.

"Thank you." She made her way over to the seating area.

"Miss Kensington, this is an unexpected surprise."

"Miss Ryan, hello. I'm sorry for intruding on you like this

but I wanted to talk to you before you left for Liverpool."

"Well I was just going for a walk; you're welcome to join me."

The two girls left the hotel and made their way towards the Tower Bridge. When the hotel was out of sight Amanda said, "Miss Ryan what I have to say concerns my uncle and by all accounts your father."

"Please," Chelsey interrupted, "call me Chelsey."

Amanda smiled, "Chelsey, I saw Daniel last night and I've never seen him so upset before. He tried to call you and your mum this morning but you had left your rooms. He left a message for you."

"I only just got the message. He must have called whilst we were having breakfast."

"Well Daniel told me the whole story about you and your mum and what happened. I wasn't as surprised as he thought I'd be. You see I'd found a photo of your mum along with his wedding ring one day a few years back when I first started working for him. Before that all I knew was something big happened before I was born between him and his family. He hasn't been on talking terms to my mum much for a long time. When he told me the story things started to make sense. He doesn't want you guys to go home without seeing you again. He really does still love your mum and he says he wants to get to know you."

By now they had walked about half way across Tower Bridge. They stopped and watched the boats going up and down the Thames for a while.

Amanda broke the silence, "Do you think your mum wants to see him again?"

"I think so but at the moment she is trying to make sense of everything. She went for walk this morning to sort things out in her head. I'm not sure where she is."

"If we organised somewhere for them to meet, do you think you could talk her into being there?"

"I probably could. I'm not promising anything. I won't really know until I see her later but give me a time and place and I'll do my best."

They sat thinking about it for a while. "Why not meet right here?" Amanda suggested. "It's lovely here. Maybe around seven this evening."

"Sounds good."

They got up and walked back towards the hotel. When the hotel came in sight Amanda turned to Chelsey and said, "I've just realised something. If Dan is my uncle and your father then that makes us cousins doesn't it."

Chelsey thought about this for a moment, "Yes I guess it does. Congrats you are the first cousin I've ever had." They both laughed.

"See you at seven." Amanda said as she headed for her car.

"See you later."

Jackie hadn't said a lot about her walk that morning or what conclusions she had come to about Daniel, so Chelsey figured she was still figuring things out. She decided against telling her that she had met up with Amanda and that they had organised to meet up again that evening, for the time being anyway. She didn't want to put pressure on her to make a quick decision. At half past six Jackie and Chelsey finished their dinner and headed out of the restaurant.

"It's a lot nicer in there when it isn't so packed." Jackie remarked.

"Yes, you don't have to wait so long for your food to come." They sat down in the corner of the lobby beside the window. "Do you fancy going for a walk?" Chelsey asked, "It's a nice evening."

"Umm, nah. I'm comfy here." Jackie snuggled down into her seat. "I feel like going to sleep."

"I feel like going for a walk."

"Well go on then, don't let me stop you." Jackie closed her eyes.

"I don't want to go on my own." Jackie made no comment. She tried again. "Come on please. Walk off that strawberry cheesecake you had." Jackie opened one eye. "Please. You'll thank me for it later."

"Ok if you insist."

Chelsey smiled and jumped up. Jackie got up more slowly with a quiet groan. "Oh, the things I do for you."

Chelsey linked arms with her mum. "You love me really." She teased. She decided to tell her that Daniel would be there as they got closer to the rendezvous place. She hoped that Amanda was having just as an easy time with Daniel.

After finishing his dinner Daniel sat down at his desk and started studying his schedule for the weeks ahead. He had another show at the end of the week in London and then he had three in Paris at the beginning of August. He had a few things to finish off for the show at the end of the week and then check that all the travel arrangements for the flight to Paris had been confirmed. Some of his team were flying out two weeks after the London show and the rest of the crew were flying out two days later. He had three shows in Paris on consecutive nights, the 2nd, 3rd and 4th August. They had Monday the 5th off and then on Tuesday they were all flying back to London. They had a quiet few weeks – quiet in that they didn't have any shows – until they flew out to Milan on the 3rd of September for two shows that weekend.

Daniel ran a hand through his hair. He couldn't concentrate. He put the schedule back in his draw and sat starring at the wall. Amanda had told him about meeting up with Chelsey and the rendezvous they had organised. He was worried that Jackie wouldn't come. Chelsey hadn't sounded so confidant. He was so engrossed in his thoughts that he didn't hear the tap on the door. He jumped when someone tapped him on the shoulder.

"Sorry I didn't mean to scare you." Amanda said. "Are you ready to go?"

"I think so. Do you think they will come?"

"I hope so. But if you don't go you will never know."

When Amanda and Daniel arrived at the Bridge it was a little after seven. Chelsey and Jackie were nowhere to be seen. They waited for a few minutes. Daniel kept looking at his watch.

"Don't panic yet Dan; they may be on their way." Amanda sincerely hoped they were. She had never seen him this affected by anything. She tried to distract him by talking about how well the shows had gone but he didn't want to talk. Ten minutes later Daniel was ready to go. He was sure that he had been stood up. He was just about to go when he saw Jackie and Chelsey in the distance walking toward them.

Chelsey saw him and Amanda in the distance and decided to tell Jackie before Jackie saw them and got another shock. "By the way mum, Daniel is just up ahead, he wanted to see you again before we went home."

Jackie looked up the path and stopped when she saw him and Amanda. She turned to Chelsey, "Who organised this?"

"Me and Amanda did, I met her this morning after you went for a walk. She told me that Daniel wanted to see you again. Go talk to him mum please." Chelsey urged.

Jackie hesitated.

"He still loves you. He really does. I don't know him at all mum but I'll never get to know him if you don't talk to him again."

Jackie thought about this for a moment. "I suppose you're right." She said. They walked the last few steps toward Daniel and Amanda.

"Hello." Daniel said.

"Hi." Amanda said. She nodded to Chelsey and the two girls discreetly left them to talk. Jackie leaned against the railings and looked down at the river.

Daniel pushed his chair next to her. He took her hand. "I still love you Jackie. I don't want to lose you again. If you can find it in your heart to forgive me, maybe we can try and be a family again."

"I'd like that. I never stopped loving you, even when I thought you were dead." She threw her arms around his neck and he embraced her back. "So what is your story, I never did hear it."

Daniel told her his story.

"That night I took the car and drove to the nearest pub. I was just going to go in and have a few beers and calm down. I wasn't mad at you I was mad at myself for not being able to get a job and able to give you what you deserved. I wanted children as much as you did. I just wasn't thinking straight. I thought if I went out and cleared my head it would be ok. When I got out of the car at the pub I must have dropped the keys on the ground. When I got to the door of the pub I heard the roar of an engine. I looked around to see some guy had gotten into the car and was driving off. I ran after him and cut him off but he just ran right over me.

The next thing I remember was waking up in hospital two weeks later. I couldn't remember a thing. I had a total mental block. Worse than that I was paralyzed from the waist down. I couldn't handle it. It took me over a year to accept my lot and slowly my memory came back. I was desperate to see you but I couldn't find you. I went back to you mum and dads but they must have moved. I didn't know what happened to you or the baby. I didn't even know if you had a boy or a girl until Chelsey walked into my hotel room. Then I started thinking that you would be better off without me. You deserved better than a cripple in a wheelchair. I patched things up with my parents. They apologised for not telling you I was alive and wanted to help me out as much as they could. It's a long story. Anyway I moved back home and they encouraged me to take up sketching again. So I did and that's how I got into designing dresses. My mum made up my first design on her sewing machine and I bribed a friend to wear it to the theatre. The Daily Mail newspaper was there and somebody took a photo of her. She was in the paper the next day under the heading, 'The Best Dressed Girl at the Panto.' The paper wanted to know where she got the dress from and as they say the rest is history.

I couldn't believe it when Chelsey turned up and started going on about you. I was scared that she wasn't who she said she was. I was scared that if I did find you after all this time you'd be with someone else and you wouldn't want me."

Jackie bent down and kissed him on the lips. "There will never be anyone else but you." She said.

Amanda and Chelsey strolled back towards them and arrived just at this point.

"I don't believe it." Amanda said when she saw them kissing. Chelsey couldn't either but she was too happy to speak. Tears ran down her face. Never in her life did she think it was possible for her mum and dad to get back together. When Jackie looked up and saw her, Chelsey walked towards them.

"You've a daughter to get to know." Jackie said to Daniel. Daniel looked up at Chelsey with a smile.

"You've a niece to get to know too." Daniel beckoned Amanda over. Chelsey gave Jackie a hug. She then gave Daniel a hug. Jackie and Chelsey were crying and laughing at the same time. Amanda stood on the outside of the circle until Daniel pulled her into the group.

"You're family too." He said. By way of an introduction Jackie gave her a hug. It wasn't long before she was crying too. The wind picked up a bit so Daniel suggested they all head home. They all piled into Daniel's car and headed back to his apartment.

Chapter Twenty Four

When Chelsey awoke the next morning she had to pinch herself to make sure that the last twenty-four hours hadn't been a dream. The first thing she did that morning was phone her grandparents and tell them the news; of course they were thrilled about it. She then phoned Jason, Phil and Annie and told them.

Breakfast that morning was like nothing she had ever had before and she wouldn't forget it for a long time. They talked and laughed and told each other stories of the past.

The next few days past in a flurry of activity. Jackie and Daniel both wanted to go away and spend sometime on their own. They had so much to catch up on. It was arranged that Jackie and Daniel would fly over to Ireland the day after the last show in Paris and spend a few weeks together before flying to Milan. Chelsey, Jack, Christine, Jason, Phil and Annie were all invited to be special guests at his shows in Paris.

After the final show in Paris, Daniel and his staff and his family along with Jason, Phil, Annie, Jack and Christine were sitting in the hotel bar having a celebratory drink, like they do after every final night. Amanda sat down next to Chelsey and said,

"Daniel phoned my mum the day after he and your mum made up. They haven't really spoken to each other in twenty years. They patched things up and they are coming to the Milan show as special guests. I have you to thank for that." Amanda explained.

"Me, I didn't do anything. I didn't even know your mum and Daniel weren't speaking to each other." Chelsey said.

"Well if you hadn't walked onto that catwalk in Liverpool and nearly messed up the show, your mum and dad wouldn't have gotten back together and he and my mum wouldn't have forgiven each other now. So thank you."

"You're welcome. I didn't know that messing up Daniel's show would do so much good."

"Well next time you plan on walking down the catwalk you will let us know so poor Justine won't have heart failure."

"I'll do that."

After returning to London, Jack, Christine, Chelsey and Jason all went to the airport to see Daniel and Jackie off as they flew out to Ireland. That day was a turning point not only in their lives but also in Chelsey's life and in Jack and Christine's lives.

Chelsey realised that she could now forget about her past and move on. She had the family she always wanted and she had the answers to all her questions. All her worries and concerns had melted away.

Jack and Christine also felt the burden of guilt lift off their shoulders. The enormous sense of relief washed over them like a wave. All the skeletons in the closet had been let out. No more secrets would prick at their conscience.

As the plane taxied down the runway and took off, the four of them walked back to the car. Jason walked slowly so Jack and Christine would get ahead of them. When they were out of earshot he caught hold of Chelsey's arm and kissed her on the lips. Chelsey raised and eyebrow and smiled,

"What was that for?"

"I've been wanting to do that for a while. May I buy you dinner sometime?"

"You mean like in a fancy restaurant instead of fish and chips from the chippy."

"Absolutely. With your dad being rich and famous I can't very well take his daughter to just any old place can I, I don't think he would be impressed."

Chelsey laughed, "Oh so it's my dad you're trying to impress and I thought it was me you were trying to impress." She kissed him back.

Jason put his arm around her shoulders and they followed Jack and Christine out to the car.

Written by Hannah Sellars

Lightning Source UK Ltd.
Milton Keynes UK
15 July 2010
157064UK00009B/7/P